The Follower

The Follower

Michael M. Kohler

XULON PRESS

Xulon Press
2301 Lucien Way #415
Maitland, FL 32751
407.339.4217
www.xulonpress.com

Cover design and photography:
Marcello Aquino / Triple7creative
Model: Marcello Aquino

Printed in the United States of America.

ISBN-13: 978-1-6312-9025-1

Dedication

This book is dedicated, first and foremost, to my wonderful Savior, Yeshua the Messiah; in whom I express an unbelievable gratitude for giving His life in my place! To my two wonderful boys, Matthew and Levi, who have encouraged me through it all. This book is also dedicated to *all True Followers* of the Kingdom of God.

Table of Contents

Acknowledgements

I would like to thank the following people for all of their hard work in proof-reading, valuable insight, and their prayers: Dori Albright Cass, Emily Carlascio, Sharon Stotts, Lance and Shani Hamel, Maria Mendoza Rodriguez, and to all my other friends and family who have encouraged me along the way! Thank you all!

Special thanks to Rabbi Yossef Wentz for guidance in all things pertaining to Jewish content.

Special thanks to Victoria Elam for the many hours of hard work helping to promote and get my book out.

Special shout out to the most awesome graphic designer of all time… Marcello Aquino. Great cover design!

Introduction

This book was written in order to challenge us *all* to step up our dedication to following God! Our Father has called us out from the world... to be a light! Can we *be* that light if we look just like the world? A lot of modern-day Christianity has lessened the seriousness of following Yeshua. There's no longer any *discipline*. Notice the root word of discipline... Do you see the word *disciple* in it?

Salvation is a gift, in all of it wonder and glory; but if we don't *maintain* that gift... it won't be effective in our life, or the lives around us! Paul says in Philippians 2:12

So then, my beloved, just as you have always obeyed, not as in my presence only, but now much more in my absence, ***work out your salvation with fear and trembling****.*

Maintain your walk with God! Take it seriously! If you read all of chapter 2 in Philippians, you will find an in-depth look at how we are to do that. Remember, Yeshua is the example we are to follow! In *HIS* strength... we can achieve a stronger witness in this world! We are all commanded to...

"Go into all the world and preach the gospel to all creation. These signs will accompany those who have believed: in My name they will cast out demons, they will speak with new tongues; they

will pick up serpents, and if they drink any deadly poison, it will not hurt them; they will lay hands on the sick, and they will recover."

Mark 16:15-18

In my next book, ***The Discipler,*** Benjamin will continue his adventure in the present-day world; operating in the power of The Ruach *HaKodesh*...The Holy Spirit! He will teach many, the ways of Yeshua. He, and others, will fight against the evil that has spread across the globe because of Satan's last attempt to keep control of this world! Twists and turns, as well as danger and victory will be intertwined with the miraculous signs and wonders that follow!

Thank you for being a part of my journey!
Michael

Chapter 1: The End

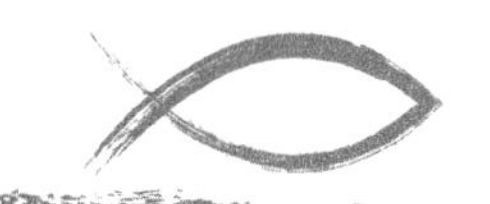

The darkness behind my eyelids was nowhere equal to the black hole consuming my will to exist. My senses were piqued though, and every heartbeat was pounding in my head like a bass drum. The aroma of hundred-dollar scotch lingered in my nose as I brought the glass of Balvenie to my lips. I paused for a moment… savoring its bouquet, while the melodic chime of ice cubes resounded in my ears.

My heart was cold, black, and unfeeling; save hatred. It's been two years to the day since I lost my family, and I have prepared a requiem for myself. It took one full year to be able to walk on my own again, and another to realize there was no point in it! These last few months have been little more than a feeble existence. My friends stopped calling and I haven't heard a knock on the door in days. The only proof of an occupant in this dark, dank hovel is the delivery boxes, cartons, and canisters that have accumulated throughout the living room and kitchen.

Here's to you Ben. I thought, while downing another swill of scotch. *Two years without Sarah and the children.* My stomach groaned; not from the alcohol churning my empty gut, but from the anger rising within me. I have spent most of my life dedicated to the study of scriptures and its translations. I have been an affluent member of the Linguistics Society of America and a tenured Professor of Hebrew Linguistics at Penn State University.

Where in my life have I failed so miserably as to deserve God turning His back on me?

"I hate you." I whispered.

My thoughts flashed back to that horrible night.

The wipers were hypnotic, and the rain beating against the windshield numbed my senses considerably. The headlights illuminated every raindrop caught in its path, like thousands of liquid sparks bouncing off the road. It provided little in the way of guidance between the lines on the highway, and everything beyond the scope of my headlights was even worse. *I have two more hours of this. If I could stand her relentless nagging, I'd wake Sarah so she could help me stay awake*. Our marriage was normally, quite amazing, but for some reason, this weekend had brought out the worst in both of us! I thought twice about waking her. One heated argument after another this weekend put a kibosh on *that* idea! I'd rather prop my eyelids open with toothpicks and sit on broken glass for the rest of the trip! *Just ten more miles to the next exit and a cup of Java... I can make it that far.*

Monotony found its place in my reality. My awareness became dreamlike, making it difficult to discern between what was real and what was not. My eyes started to close while my mind convinced me that just a few seconds of this would be ok. Sleep was just *soooo* inviting. The sound of the rain, the mechanical whirr of the wipers, and the defrost blowing hot air on my face was far too relaxing; but the slumber was soon shattered. The sound of a loud horn blasting, and a blinding light shot through me as everything exploded; like being in a champagne bottle thrown against a wall!

My vehicle spun around like a top then tumbled end over end with glass and other objects flying everywhere! I blacked out.

When I came to, there was mayhem all around. People were screaming above loud machinery, and I could just make out the flash of emergency lights through my swollen eyelids. I tried to open them, but I couldn't . . . in fact, I couldn't move anything. I was strapped down to a backboard and being lifted onto a gurney. *What happened?* With all I could muster up, I screamed,

"What's going on? Where is my family?" No one was responding! "Please! Where are my wife and kids?" Immediately, I heard a benevolent female voice tell me

"Try to stay calm Mr. Messler; you are going to be okay. We are transporting you to Mercy Medical in Rochester." Before I could ask any more questions, I slipped from consciousness and woke two weeks later in the hospital . . . without them.

My family died that night, so closing this chapter in my life is the only option I have left. The pills stuck to my tongue as I hesitated, cherishing the thought of ending this hell. I drank down the last of the scotch and breathed deeply as I laid my head back. I never thought I could take my own life, but what does it matter? Is there a Heaven? Is there a Hell? It's all just relative. I'm already living in Hell; the real one can't be any worse!

Within just minutes, my head began to spin out of control!

Wow . . . This is working a lot faster than I expected! My body felt numb, and my life *DID* actually flash before my eyes in a strobe like fashion. It was over in seconds, but every memory I took with me was vivid and colorful.

Weightlessness shrouded me. It felt as if I were floating; suspended in darkness. I embraced the comfort I found in it, yet . . . I longed for my family. To spend eternity with them was all I wanted. Was I meant to exist without them? Was my punishment to float aimlessly with just the memory of them dying at my hand? The moment *that* realization took hold of me, the comfort I briefly experienced, dissipated... and I began falling... plummeting through this unknown expanse. I could feel the force of gravity increase by the second. It ended with a body breaking impact! It felt as if every bone in my body was fractured, and the air was knocked out of me! As soon as I was able to suck in a breath of air... dust was all I took in. It choked out my lungs and sent me into a coughing fit. When recovered, I sat up slowly, feeling my limbs and thankful to find them intact. What kind of drug induced, psychedelic, binge-drinking alternate reality had I landed in? This was just too strange to comprehend! I stood to my feet... stretched... and attempted to massage away the pain.

It was night, but a full moon provided plenty light to make out some of my surroundings. I could smell the faint aroma of something familiar in the air; olive trees in bloom, I thought... and the raw earthy smell of the country. No city smells or sounds of traffic. This must be a side effect brought on by the drugs, alcohol, and my timely death. However, it seemed real enough.

I brushed myself off and tried to gather my bearings. I had no idea where I was exactly, or which way to go from here. It was evident that I was standing in the middle of a small dirt road, so I had only one of two choices... right, or left. I turned to the left and allowed the moon to guide me. There were rolling hills and trees scattered about the countryside and no sound but that of a few insects singing their night song. After walking for a while, fatigue overcame me, and the chill of the night began to set in my bones. Finding an adequate tree for shelter, I gathered my arms around my body to keep warm and found a neat little nook between some roots to bed down for the night. For a dead person, I sure could *feel* the cold. If this was a dream – I was still cold!

Chapter 2: The Beginning

Somewhere between the folds of dreams and reality, I heard voices and felt someone kick me in the ribs! It angered me and I jumped up into a defensive stance, ready to face my assailants! There before me were two men in Middle Eastern attire staring at me. They stepped back, surprised at first, and then one spoke to me in a slight variance of the Aramaic language that I was unfamiliar with. It was kind of like trying to understand someone with a deep southern accent. It can be done.... It was just a little more difficult.

"Who are you...what... what is this you are wearing? Where are you from, foreigner?" I responded the closest version of the language I could simulate...

"I am an American, and I'm not really sure how I got here or where I am." They both stared at me for a moment, pondering what to do about this *strange* man. They muttered something quietly to each other and turned to leave.

"Wait!" I shouted. "Where am I? Can you help me find my way to the nearest city, or a place where I can make a phone call?" The older man turned and scowled at me.

"Your feet will find their way soon enough – now go! Go back to your own people!" They looked me over from head to toe, spat in my direction, then turned and went on their way.

I looked down at my clothes and wondered why they found them so offensive. I spent two and a half years traveling back and forth between Haifa and Jerusalem studying in their universities and was never rebuked because of my clothing. I had on a button up flannel shirt, 501 blue jeans and a pair of boots. I may be a little outdated, but I just chalked it up to being the eccentric, educated type. I watched as the two men disappeared into the dawn and leaving me alone to ponder my situation.

The daylight brought with it more revelation as to my whereabouts. I was definitely in Israel or Jordan… maybe near the Golan Heights. I had been through this area many times before but found it strangely different now. It seemed so remote. I turned westward again and continued my quest for civilization.

Miles fell beneath my feet before I finally came to a conclusion concerning my predicament. I was one hundred percent certain that I was totally, unequivocally, irrefutably clueless as to what was going on! I had no answers and could only wish this nightmare to be over. My mind was wallowing in self-pity when I heard a distant voice behind me yelling.

"Wait! Wait for me!"

I turned and looked behind me to find a man running to catch up with me. He looked to be a young man of about seventeen to twenty years old; tall and dark complected with a mass of curly black hair and a patchy beard. His clothing was modest, yet well-tailored... showing evidence of some wealth and prestige. Although confident, he retained an air of innocence as that of a much younger man.

Puffs of dust rose from the dirt road as each one of his feet made contact with the powdery surface. Breathing hard, he came along side me. Supporting himself with his hands on his knees, he looked up at me and grinned.

"You are an odd man!" He paused to catch his breath again.

"I had to catch up to you and see for myself what manner of man this is and where he comes from! May I travel with you? We are, it seems, going the same way."

His deep brown eyes were wide with excitement and his bright smile infectious. I struggled with an explanation for my appearance. Maybe I can just avoid it altogether.

"My name is Ben, Benjamin Messler. Traveling with you would be better than traveling alone. I have no idea as to where I am."

"I am Simon, son of Josiah, I am returning home from business in Korazim on my way to Tiberias." *Finally, a city name that I recognize!* "As to where you are... you are now just north of the Sea of Galilee; your speech is strange. Where are you from?"

"I am an American professor from the state of Pennsylvania, but I studied for a brief time here in Haifa and Jerusalem as well. I am a Linguist." The look on his face said it all. The lines in his brow faded and the same silly grin took hold.

"You are an odd man! Come... we have half a day's journey and the heat of the day is already upon us."

"What were you doing in Korazim?" I said, trying to make polite conversation.

"My father has vineyards there and we are providing wine for a wedding feast in Cana. You are most welcome in our home and to a proper change of clothes if you like. My family will not believe me if I tell them the story of such a strange man without presenting you to them so they may see for themselves."

He shook his head and chuckled at the thought of his family's reaction when they see me.

Everything up to this point had been difficult to assess, but I was beginning to understand a few things. This is not modern-day Israel.

The clothing.

The language.

The lack of modern roads and transportation.

Furthermore, this is not a dream. I never *sleep* in a dream. In fact, I spent a long, cool night sleeping under a tree that was very real.

Am I dead? That is the only explanation worth believing at this point, except the fact that my feet are killing me, and we still have a half a day's journey ahead of us.

What I wouldn't give for an air-conditioned taxi and an ice-cold glass of Coke!

"We are close to my father's," said Simon. "This olive tree orchard is the beginning of our land. We have only a short way to go."

The property was literally breathtaking. The olive tree blossoms were the most beautiful I'd ever seen....and the fragrance was captivating. The modern world has all but destroyed the natural goodness God intended for the Earth to offer. Fertilizers, pesticides and GMO's have become the wave of the future and have succeeded in ruining the natural order of things.

"Your father must be wealthy," I said. "This orchard is very large."

"Oh yes. Our family has been blessed for many generations. Someday, this will all be mine. I am the first born of nine brothers. Therefore, I have the greatest responsibility." A moment later we were hailed by a servant attending the orchard near the house.

"Master! Your father is expecting you and I was told to direct you to the olive presses. He is there now."

"Very good Gehazi! I will find him, and I will be sure and tell him of all your hard work. I would not like to see you receive any more lashes across your back because of your laziness." Simon and the servant laughed together as they embraced.

"Meet my new friend. Gehazi... this is Ben."

Gehazi looked at me with questions that I am sure puzzled him, but he immediately averted his eyes and bowed in greeting.

"Please find a house servant and tell them to prepare a place for our guest to bathe and rest from our long journey... oh, and some proper clothes for him. My brother Alpheus is of the same stature, his clothes should do well for him. Also, make certain the servants hold their tongue as you have concerning our guest's appearance." The servant was all business now as he bowed to Simon and took off running for the house. "He and I grew up together and are good friends but he knows his place."

As I was thinking about that bath and a nap, we came around a building to find his father, busy at work alongside the servants.

"No, no, no... you must first wedge the stone here, before you start work on the other side."

His father was a large man with a gruff voice...quite intimidating. He was dressed in a rich man's garments, but undeterred by the work he was performing. As he put down the tool he was working with, I couldn't help but notice how big his hands were. They dwarfed mine, and the calluses from years of hard work were quite noticeable. This man was rich but was not afraid to get his hands dirty. He turned to face us as Simon hailed him. My eyes were met with a very soft and gentle gaze. It's easy to see that this family is very respectable, honorable and hard working.

"Father, this is my new friend Benjamin, whom I met on the road back from Korazim. I invited him to stay with us for a time."

"Well, an interesting sort you are. Are you from Rome? A soldier perhaps? My son is always bringing home strays, and your story would not be the first lie I've heard!" He laughed with a barrel-chested roll and embraced me with a bear hug. "I am Josiah, of the tribe of Asher." Lifting me off the ground, he boomed "You are welcome in my home Benjamin, but if you steal from me or run off with one of my daughters, I will have your head!" That last comment really settled in and took root.

"Thank you for being so gracious... and you will have no problems from me. I would like to keep my head."

"I like this one Simon!" Josiah slapped me on the back, almost sending me to the ground. "Get him to the house so you both may rest before the festivities begin. We are having a banquet this evening. You like food don't you Benjamin? As you can see by my girth, I am always looking for a reason to celebrate with food!" Simon escorted me to the house where a servant was waiting for us. Simon gave her more instructions then I was led upstairs to my room.

My accommodations were, to say the least, very nice. The room was small, but had a balcony overlooking the courtyard, and beyond that, the orchard we'd walked through. There was a small bed, a wooden bench, and a table in the corner. There sat upon it a basin of fresh water with flower petals in it.

The sun was sinking lower over the hills to the west, and a warm, orange glow painted the tops of the flowering trees in the orchard. It was so magical.... like something out of a fairy tale. The trees seemed to shiver with delight at the expected coolness of the night followed by the kiss of dew in the morning. *This could be heaven,* I thought. I felt content enough to live in this moment for the rest of eternity. This was the most peace I'd encountered in a long time now. Pain was not far away though, it lingered just below the surface; like a splinter, festering and infecting my soul.

My heart sank into a deep depression. I craved sleep, so I lay down on the bed and drifted into a dreamless sleep.

A gentle hand shook me.

"My master has requested that I wake you. You will dine with him shortly. Here is a tunic, robe, sash and sandals for you." He stepped back, bowed and gracefully extended his hand in the direction of the basin. "You will find fresh water to bathe with on the table over here."

"Thank you. Tell your master I am coming."

As the door shut behind him, I quickly took off my modern clothing and washed myself. I laid out my new clothes with a little bit of reluctance. It consisted of; my undergarment, called a tunic, the mantle, which was the outer garment, and a wide leather belt. I compared the difference between my underwear and the tunic. I'm sorry, but *Fruit of the Loom* would win out in the area of comfort in this situation; not to mention the technical savvy it's going to take to put the tunic on correctly. *No one would know if I were wearing my underwear* I thought. *I could get away with it* – however, I must make an attempt to fit in here. In spite of my reluctance, I put them on. Everything fit surprisingly well, but the sandals were a bit small for my feet. I tied them up as loosely as I could and shuffled down to meet my hosts – I miss my underwear already.

My evening was spent with a very large and happy family. "John and Kate Makes Eight" had nothing on this multitude. There were ten boys ranging from two to eighteen years old, and three daughters that were close to marrying age. This was made obvious by the way they were checking out the young men in the crowd.

They were giggling and sharing their thoughts on each prospect in the room as they stood by their father, serving him his food and drink. I couldn't help but think how much things have changed. Trying to get one of my own children to serve *me* with food or drink would be met with a resounding cry of excuses and a quick disappearing act.

The servants were many… and very busy keeping the others well fed. The wine goblets were filled long before they could be emptied. Josiah and his wife, Rachel, were outstanding hosts. They had invited at least twenty or more friends to the banquet, and all were having a wonderful time. I, on the other hand, found myself very overwhelmed. I was introduced to every family member and friend and was met with a lot of questions concerning my "accent". I changed the subject and put the focus back on *them*. It worked more often than not, but in the process, exhausted every ounce of mental capacity I could ration.

I finally withdrew to a place to eat and found my appetite waning. As I pondered having another drink, Simon reclined on the couch beside me. It seemed as if he were trying to take inventory of my thoughts before speaking. He was having a hard time reading my countenance.

"Are you not enjoying yourself Ben? You've not touched your food; although, the wine has not been far from your lips all evening." He was right, and my head was reeling from the effects of it.

"Really good wine." I toasted him and emptied the cup.

"You are so quiet. Please, tell me about yourself. In our conversations earlier, you would not go into detail about where you are from. Why is that?"

My evasiveness was not fair to the only friend I had in this time zone, so I motioned to a servant to fill me up again and began my story… at least part of it.

"Simon, you wouldn't believe half of what I tell you, but I can start with this . . . you and your family has shown me more kindness in a day, than many of my own friends showed me in a year's time. I am very thankful for that."

Simon smiled and nodded. For such a young man, he had a maturity about him that was beyond his years. This is a young man, of course, who wasn't raised on video games and movie channels. Life was more meaningful here, and this was no microwave society where everything was instantaneous and entertaining. Hard work was an everyday staple; you grow soft… and you don't eat. I could safely assume that Simon had probably been working from the time he could walk. Now he sits next to me, a man half my age, and *he* shows *me* a maturity level higher than my own. I realized then, how much healing I needed. Talking to him could be the first step. I drew in a deep breath and began.

"Simon, my wife and children died two years ago." The words caught in my throat, choking me, as I spoke about their deaths for the first time. "It's been very difficult without them in my life, and there isn't a day that goes by that I don't wish I could change what happened. It was all my fault."

There, I said it… those words that I had been thinking, but not saying; those words that had been haunting me for years. They filled every second of every day without letting up; and the moment I spoke them was the beginning of a breakthrough in my life. Tears began to well up in my eyes as Simon sat up and put his arm around my shoulder.

"Grief is a very difficult thing, but this is something we all must face in our lifetime. I'm sorry that it came so soon for you. It's hard for some to accept your grieving or understand what you are going through. Perhaps your friends were unable to help, not because they didn't want to, but because they didn't know *how* to." Every time Simon opens his mouth, I am amazed at the wisdom he displays.

"Now, tell me about where you come from. Is it Rome, like my father said? Perga? Tarsus? Come... you must tell me. You don't look like a Gentile, but you were wearing clothing we are unaccustomed to seeing here in Israel. Are you Jewish?"

"My family *is* Jewish, although my father and mother have not lived in Israel for many years. I was born in a country like Rome, very far away. It is a land I am sure you haven't heard of." I felt sorry for Simon. He tried so hard to wrap his mind around what I was saying, but now seemed a little hesitant to ask any more questions. "As far as what I do... I am a teacher of languages. I am a Linguist."

"You surprise me Benjamin! A Rabbi?"

"Not exactly a Rabbi. I *have* studied the Torah extensively, but I am not a Rabbi. I am a Linguist. I teach Hebrew, Aramaic, and Greek, but more specifically, Semitic Linguistics and Bible Philology." Again – the look on his face said *"sorry I asked"* and reminded me how strange this all must sound to him.

Simon turned his attention to another bite of food and spoke again, this time with his mouth full.

"You must come to Cana with us in the morning. Weddings are always an exciting event. Will you come with us?"

Without hesitation I said "Yes – and if you would allow me to – I would like to help out in some way to repay you for your hospitality." In one respect, I dreaded the thought of more exposure to this strange new world – because I felt so out of place – but I was obligated to pay back Simon and his family for their selfless generosity.

"There will be much to do. The feast will begin in two days. This is the reason I went to Korazim… to secure more wine for the wedding. Our supply is limited here, so we have to make up the difference from the vineyards over there. My Uncle is a difficult man, so everything must be perfect for his son's wedding. We could use your help… thank you Ben."

I was exhausted, and the thought of *another* journey on foot made me even more tired. I haven't had this much exercise in over two years, unless you count walking back and forth from the Lazy Boy to the bedroom. "Forgive me, but I have to sleep off this wine in my head if we are leaving in the morning."

"You will sleep well tonight, I'm sure. We leave at dawn. I will have a servant prepare you for the passage to Cana, and provide you with some different garments for the wedding." Simon looked down at my feet. "I'm sorry Benjamin. Your feet are rather large" Simon laughed. "We will get you a new pair in the morning."

I was grateful for that, but more traveling? I was tired just thinking about walking on a dusty, dirt road with no socks. I said goodnight and excused myself to my room.

As my thoughts drifted toward the wedding feast, memories of my own came flooding back. Now, even with alcohol numbing my senses, I can't help but think about it. Back home . . . back in my *old* life . . . my *real* life . . . my . . . *whatever* . . . drinking kept all those emotions at bay. *Why is this happening to me?* All I wanted to do was be rid of my miserable life, and everything keeps circling me right back around to it – even in a life thousands of years before I was ever born. *God has a terrible sense of humor.*

I lay on my bed and looked up at the cracks in the ceiling. Fluid shapes changed with the movement of a single flame, burning from the oil lamp in my room. Ghostly images were dancing – mocking me. I breathed a heavy sigh and turned on my side – ignoring the demons from my past.

Tears burned my skin as they ran down my face again, leaving a pool of emotion on the linen beneath me. For the first time in many years – I prayed. *God, you know how I feel about You. It appears You are the cause of all my pain. I can't turn to anyone, or anything else. Nothing is pulling me out of this hell You've put me in. If You are there... please, help me.*

I fell asleep to the sound of my own child-like whimpers – not knowing how much that small prayer was being answered – long before I ever prayed it.

Chapter 3: New Friends, New Wine

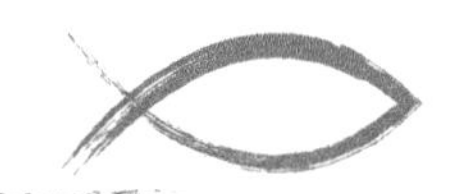

Dawn came early – *way* too early. In fact, it was still dark when a noise outside woke me. I got up and went to the balcony overlooking the courtyard. Servants were busy loading up supplies on carts.

It reminded me of the family vacations we took when I was young. My father had a knack for packing a lot into, and on top of, our old seventy- two Volvo station wagon. It was a miracle that there were any seats left to sit in when he got through. It made me smile.

I dressed and made my way down to the courtyard. The sky was beginning to show color. Dark blue on blue – fading to the hint of a golden hue touching the horizon. The air was cool and moist. I felt as if *I* were the one being gently kissed with the morning dew; just as I had imagined the orchard would be this morning. I closed my eyes and drank in this moment. *Is this what peace feels like?* Simon approached me with haste.

"Ben . . . Benjamin! Are you ready? Did you sleep well my friend?" *Ugggh . . . He was even chipper before the sun was up*. I, on the other hand, desperately needed a cup of coffee and the Wall Street Journal in my hands. "You look rested!" He lied.

"Yes, I do feel rested – for the first time in a very long while."

"Good my friend. We only have a short road ahead of us, but there will be much work when we arrive in Cana."

I was starting to look forward to the wedding in Cana. This whole situation was beginning to look like a documentary for the History Channel called "Lifestyles of the Ancient Israelites."

I had, to this point, failed to look objectively, while living among these wonderful people. I was beginning to feel a little pride in my heritage again, which had been extinguished over the years. With my background, I was only too familiar with all this. This was my line of work – my specialty. I ought to be able to blend in like a covert spy – undercover and unsuspected. Aside from my own childhood and Jewish upbringing; my studies, as an adult, have been varied but quite extensive. I can quote scripture in Greek, Hebrew, and various forms of Aramaic. Their customs are well known to me; so I should endeavor to fit in, and not look like a man from the twentieth century. Simon approached me again – this time with a child in tow.

"Ben, this is my little brother Samuel. He has asked to walk with us men instead of in the back with the woman and children." Samuel couldn't contain his excitement.

"I will keep up! You'll see. I am strong, and I don't whine like my other brothers."

Simon talked to me out of the side of his mouth, as if to hide his words from Samuel.

"This is my *shadow*. My little brother strives to be just like me. Not long ago, he received the rod from my father for cutting the beard off one of our best goats. He stuck it to his face with honey and walked through the house ordering the servants around in his best, deep voice, thinking he could fool everyone . . .

The servants played along for a while, calling him *Master Simon*, but as soon as father found out what he had done, he had to correct Samuel – but not without stifling a laugh while he did it.

We all have laughed many times since then whenever father tells the story – it's one of his favorites now. Samuel is a good child, but he can get a little excitable." He turned to Samuel. "Shadow, I don't think Benjamin wants to be bothered with . . ." I cut him off.

"No, it's ok. Samuel can walk with us. I would welcome his conversation, if it will keep you from filling my ears with more of your long stories!" Samuel covered his smile with both hands and giggled, while Simon looked at me with shock. He put his hands on his hips and then proceeded to shake an accusing finger at me.

"You seemed to have found your place in this family, Benjamin. 'A good laugh, when enjoyed by two at the expense of another, is better than a lone man sharing his laughter with the wind' – as my father would say." Simon scooped up his brother and threw him over his shoulder, spinning and laughing. "You, young man, need to learn how to hold your tongue before you find yourself in the back with your sisters."

"Noooo, Simon, no! I will hold my tongue – I promise!"

"Just as I thought." Simon swung his little brother down into a hug and kissed him on the forehead before setting him on his feet. Samuel then proceeded to stick out his tongue and hold it between his fingers – trying hard not to laugh. Simon began chasing and playfully kicking Samuel in the posterior as he ran.

The distance to Cana should be about twelve miles. So by my estimates, it should only take about four to six hours to get there. Strange . . . I don't dread the thought of walking this morning near as much as I thought I would.

With the efficiency of a well-oiled machine, everything was packed and moving westward just as the sun finished cresting the horizon. Samuel now walked between Simon and me. I estimated him to be about five years old.

Just when I thought we would have a quiet morning, Samuel began with the questions. *Why this... and why that... and how come* became the topic of conversation without an end in sight. My own boy, Jacob, liked to play the "why" game relentlessly at one stage in his life. Samuel was coming in at a close second.

All of a sudden, I couldn't help but be overcome with grief. Jake was only twelve, and Emily just sixteen when they died; so young, and so full of life and promise. It wasn't fair to have their life cut so short... especially by their own father's hand. Vivid memories came at me like the Semi that took their lives. Jake was five years old again, strapped in his booster seat and bombarding me with questions.

"Daddy... Why won't Emily play trucks with me in the backyard?"

"Well Jacob, girls are like that. They'd rather play house and have tea parties. Not many *young ladies* like to play in the dirt."

"But Daddy... Why? That's so boring sittin' at a table all dressed up n' actin' silly n' stuff. That's no fun!" He crinkled his nose at the thought and then changed the subject as soon as he looked out the window. "Daddy... Why do those birds always fly like that? Is that one in the front their leader? Does he show the others where to go?"

I looked through the side window to see a flock of geese flying in a V formation. I began to share, in detail, how drafting and aerodynamics play a part, and how they take turns when the leader gets tired and falls to the back of the formation. I was pleased with my astounding explanation of migratory birds, and the uncanny ability I have in educating my children in such a fascinating, and entertaining way. Jacob failed to see any entertainment, *OR* educational value in it at all and I was met with a resounding

"Huh?"

The smug look that I had on my face disappeared. As I recovered from my wounded pride, then Jacob hit me with the big one.... You know, the *Big One;* the one that every parent fears and tries to avoid at all cost?

"Daddy... How do babies get out of their mommy's tummies?"

The blood drained from my face... beads of perspiration popped out over my whole body. My hands were slick and shaking, making it hard to grip the steering wheel. My eyes lost focus on the road as my heart made its way up my chest, through my neck, and started pounding on the back of my eyeballs! *No.... please God no.... not now. Maybe in about another twenty years but not now.... I'm not ready for this!* Jacob continued.

"Joshy said his little brother didn't want to come out, so they had to go to the hospital and let the Doctor *de.... deribber* him. Daddy... what does *deribber* mean? How do babies get *IN* their mommy's tummies? Tell me Dad... how? Dad?"

The vision of my precious little boy in the back seat faded to the last memory I had of him. Jake was sleeping with his iPod blaring in his earphones, oblivious as to what was coming. I can be thankful my family was spared the horror of the accident. The coroner said they most likely died instantly. I on the other hand, have died in agony every moment of every day for the past two years.

Samuels's questions began to fall on deaf ears as the feelings of self-pity and loathing took over my mind. Last year would have been Jake's Bar mitzvah if we had celebrated his birthday in the Jewish tradition. He would have moved from childhood into manhood.

We had a *manly* excursion of our own planned... just us. We were going to spend a week hiking and mountain climbing together; just two of us *men* in the great outdoors! We spent months in preparation with map reading, survival skills, and first aid classes. Now, he's gone, and I'm left with the memories of what could have been. Simon must have seen the transformation in my demeanor and had noticed that I was no longer responding to Samuel.

"Samuel, you are looking tired, wait here for Gehazi and ride on the cart for a while. He should be here shortly."

"Awww Simon – but."

"Do as I say Shadow, you will thank me later, trust me." Samuel hung his head down and sulked over to the side of the road, watching the caravan move slowly by and waiting for his ride. He didn't have to wait long and was soon sound asleep in the back of the ox-drawn cart. "Benjamin... What is troubling you? Did Samuel bring this upon you?"

"Yes . . . I mean . . . No . . . No, not exactly" The muscles in my neck began to relax again as I slipped back to reality. "He just reminds me of my own son when he was about Samuels age. It's difficult being around family. It's not only a reminder of how wonderful having a family is, but it's also a reminder of how much I have lost. I'm sickened by that fact more often than not. Although, since being here, I am finding it easier to deal with the pain. It doesn't last as long anymore."

"My dear brother, God has brought you here for a purpose. Do you believe that?"

"I am beginning to – for the first time in years, I prayed last night."

"The Prophet Isaiah said *It shall come to pass that before you call... I will answer.*" I finished the scripture.

"*And while they are still speaking... I will hear them.*"

"Yes Benjamin. He will answer, and He will hear." We both smiled, now deeply aware of the kindred spirit we shared.

It's funny how rebellion had eaten away so much of my love for the Word of God. The Scriptures had become nothing more than an intellectual by-product of my Jewish upbringing. They had become just words of historical significance. Now, there was a passion being stirred in me that I hadn't felt in a long time. From a young age, I had dreams of becoming a Rabbi. I loved the Law and all the significance that went with it. The ceremonies… the clothing; everything was so magical until my life changed that afternoon.

"Benny! Come down here please." I dropped my studying and went downstairs to my father, knowing what was coming. I dreaded it. For the past six months I'd been hiding the fact that I was dating a Non-Jew.

Sarah and I met when she transferred to my school. I still remember the day she walked into the classroom. I had never met a girl that could take my breath away – until then. The door opened in the middle of Mrs. Robinson's passionate synopsis on modern day economics. She showed a trace of irritation for being interrupted, but then smiled.

"We've been expecting you Sarah. Class, this is Sarah Mansfield. She just moved here all the way from San Diego California. Please make her feel welcome. Sarah . . . welcome to Lakeview. You can have this seat right over here."

She held out her hand and guided Sarah to the desk right next to Chad Winslow. *Man, I hated that guy! I had an empty seat right next to me! Why him?* He thought he was God's gift to woman, and he wasted no time laying on the charm. Sarah politely acknowledged him, and then proceeded to give him the cold shoulder. *She dissed Chad? Now I know she's the right kind of girl for me!*

All through class, I couldn't help staring at the back of her head. She had the most beautiful, silky blonde hair I'd ever seen. Every slight movement of air would cause her hair to move like a wave over my rapidly beating heart. I rehearsed in my mind, over and over again, my introduction; hoping I wouldn't freeze up and look like a mindless idiot to her.

The bell rang, cutting short the teacher's grueling epilogue. Sarah gathered up her books and placed her papers in a binder. She stood up slowly as she glanced over her class schedule. *Here's my chance*. I walked up behind her while saying a silent prayer... *Here goes*.

"Do you know where you next class is?" I said, in my sexiest, manly voice. She turned to respond, and our eyes locked. She had the most piercing blue eyes. Her tan skin was smooth and blemish-free, except for a light sprinkle of freckles on her high cheek bones. Her lips were full and shiny from the strawberry lip gloss she wore. I could smell it, mingling with the faint scent of coconut suntan lotion. As she parted her lips to speak, her teeth 'shown like a flock of sheep which had come up from washing.' *Solomon, eat your heart out*

"Hi – yeah, um – I have Mr. Foster. English; room 305?" *Ah . . . a lost lamb just waiting to be rescued*. "I am used to getting a diagram of the school's classrooms where I come from. Here they just give you a list, pat you on the back and send you on your way!"

She laughed... *Oh so cute!*

"Well, you're in luck" I said, feeling like the cat that just ate the canary. "I have Mr. Foster this period too. Would you like me to show you the way?" She smiled, and my knees went week.

"Sure. That would be great – a . . . She hesitated, her eyes darting back and forth in a questioning manner, waiting for an introduction from me. I hope I wasn't drooling.

"Oh. . . Sorry. I'm Ben. Ben Messler – and – er – welcome to Lakeview." *Way cool Ben. Stutter why don't you!*

"Thank you, Ben Messler. You are so very kind." She winked at me and curtsied – playing on the whole *niceties* thing we had going on. From that day on, we developed a friendship that was nothing short of awesome!

That relationship was about to be tested. I thought about every excuse I could come up with, but none of them would work with my father. I entered the den and found him hunched over his desk and engrossed in his work. He felt my presence.

"Benny?" He straightened up and spun around while removing his glasses. He looked at me pensively while chewing on the ear-piece of his glasses. "Benny . . . something has come to my attention that needs addressing." His eyes had a way of burning into my soul and leaving me smoldering, like a heap of ashes. "It's been brought to my attention that you have been dating a young woman from your school. Care to elaborate on this?"

Now normally, he would be ecstatic to know I was *finally* dating. I was seventeen and hadn't shown any serious interest in *anyone* my parents had picked out for me. They came from a long line of arranged marriages and expected the same for their children.

"Yes. It's true. I've been dating Sarah for about six months now. She's a wonderful girl, father. I know you would like her if you got to know her. She really wants to meet everyone."

"Is she Jewish? Have I seen her at Synagogue?" He knew the answer to that but waited for my response anyway.

"No, she's not . . . but . . ."

"No excuses Benny. We have been over this time, and time again. There are many young ladies that we have suggested for you. Your mother and I know best. I suggest you stick to the plan. You *will* marry a Jewish girl of our choosing. Trust me son, you're too young to know what's right for you, and you don't want to throw away all the hard work we have done to establish your future. And what about your schooling? I should hope you haven't changed our plans of you attending the Jewish Theological Seminary in New York."

"I'm not throwing away anything, Father! I still plan on going to JTS . . . or maybe the Ziegler School of Rabbinic Studies."

"What? That one in California? That is a progressive school! It is far from the prestige and traditions of the Jewish Theological Seminary! I won't have it! You will quit seeing this girl, and you *will* attend JTS next fall!" His face was getting red. "I'll have no more discussions with you about any of this! Furthermore, you *will* stop seeing this girl immediately! Do you understand? You will *not* disgrace our family name by spending another moment with this *goy*[1]!"

He was absolutely livid! I had been investigated, tried, and hung without any rebuttal. Case closed! I was shaking now, and anger was welling up inside me, bringing with it, the courage to stand up to him for the first time in my life.

"How dare you belittle her because she is not Jewish! You don't even know her! NO! I won't stop seeing Sarah! We love each other and want to spend the rest of our lives together! You can't tell me who to marry, or who to love!" I had never raised my voice to my father before… and I never would again.

---

[1] *Goy: Jewish name for a non-Jew*

"Get out! Live your life the way you want to, but you'll do it on your own! Get out of my house!" Tears welled up in his eyes as he said it. He hesitated, waiting to see if I would leave. Bitterness overtook me. I turned on my heels, slammed the door, and never looked back. I could hear my father through the door crying and screaming "You're dead to me! Do you hear me? You are no longer my son!"

Father died three years later, never once having contacted me. I was surprised to see him show up for my High School graduation, although, he sat quietly in the back, and left immediately following the ceremonies without saying hello *or* goodbye. I used to think it made me a stronger man – doing what I did. Years later though, I became aware; at the birth of my daughter, how wrong I was. I was weak in the way I acted. I was prideful... taking the easy way out. He only wanted the best for me; just as I would want for Emily or Jake. I would make certain to do it better than my father did. All my prior plans for college changed because of Sarah. I went on to the same college as her, studying Hebrew Linguistics at Penn State. I put becoming a Rabbi and everything else behind me.

Now here I am in the middle of Israel, two thousand years before I was born, discussing scripture for hours with a new friend and feeling like a kid again. Simon turned to me as we walked.

"Benjamin, will you . . ." His sentence was cut short, as Gehazi came running up to us screaming.

"Simon! Samuel is injured!"

"What happened?" Gehazi grabbed Simons arm and pulled him back to the rear of the caravan, explaining as they ran. I followed quickly behind them. Within minutes, I could hear Samuel's screams of pain. We found him being held by his oldest sister. Leah was trying to comfort him while giving him some wine to try and dull his pain. As I approached the scene, I could tell his leg was obviously fractured. A small piece of the bone had just broken through the skin. The leg needed setting. I told Gehazi what I needed for a makeshift traction splint and he rushed off to get the supplies. *Thank God for those Wilderness First Aid classes!*

"Simon, I need you to kneel down behind Samuel and reach around to secure the leg. Place your hands firmly on his upper leg. You must hold it securely! Do you understand?"

He did as he was told and took his place behind his little brother. Samuel was in shock and beginning to show the effects of the wine. He stopped crying and his eyes were a little glazed over. Gehazi came back with what I needed, and I fished out a leather strap.

"Samuel, listen carefully, I need you to put this strap in your mouth and bite down hard! I am going to pull on your leg to set the bone. Do you trust me?" Samuel nodded in agreement, but not without fear in his eyes. Simon interjected.

"What are you doing Benjamin?"

"Simon, I need you to trust me too! Can you do that for me? This is the only way to straighten his leg. Otherwise, he could be a cripple for the rest of his life... or even worse, he could die! The bone is fractured and has cut through the skin. If we leave it like this, it will most likely get infected and he could die from a high fever!"

"I don't understand but I will do as you say."

With that, Simon put the strap in Samuel's mouth and bore down on the leg. I poured wine on the wound... washing any dirt away and disinfecting it. Next, I grabbed his foot and ankle and pulled with all my might. Samuel screamed then passed out. I felt his leg give, saw the bone disappear from sight, and felt it move back into place.

I poured more wine over the wound then took a long drink. Simon grabbed the wineskin from me and stole a drink for himself as well. Beads of sweat were running down his face and his hands were shaking uncontrollably. He wiped the sweat out of his eyes and asked.

"Benjamin... a Rabbi *and* a Physician? I have never seen anything like this done before! Will my brother be all right?"

I finished dressing the wound with strips of cloth soaked in olive oil and tightened the straps around the splint, and then tightened the tension on the traction and checked for a pulse on his foot.

"Samuel should be fine. He needs to stay off that leg for a while... at least until harvest comes. Right now, we need to keep it elevated. Keep his leg propped up. He will need to stay off his feet, but he should heal up nicely." We carefully loaded Samuel up on the back of the cart. "The wine should keep him sleeping for a while, but he's going to be in a lot of pain when he wakes up. What happened to him?" I asked. Leah answered the question.

"My lord, Samuel was running alongside us, and was playing on some of those large rocks over there when he slipped between two of them. His leg was wedged between them when he fell, and that's when it broke. It was awful!" She was visibly shaken. Simon put his arm around her to comfort her.

"Yes, it *was* awful...." said Simon. "...and little Samuel will have a very hard time with it when he wakes up. Leah, he will need you. He always favors you when he is sick or hurting – stay with him." Leah took her place on the cart and put Samuels head on her lap. She caressed his hair while humming a soft, sweet song to him. "He is in good hands." Simon stated as he prodded the oxen into motion. "We are not far from my Uncle's home. We will be there soon. Thank you for helping us so much, Benjamin. Where did you learn such things? I have never seen anyone do what you did."

"It would be very hard to explain. Let's just say I learned some of these things from a Physician friend of mine." Simon seemed content with the answer.

Not more than an hour later, Simon hailed to me and waved me to come join him.

"Ah, look there Benjamin!" He pointed ahead of us. Just off the road to the right was his Uncle's place. "We are here at last. We will work until sundown, and the Sabbath begins. Tomorrow, we will go to the Synagogue! Will you read for us from the Scriptures?" My heart was saying yes, but my mind was saying no.

"Yes... I would love to, if it is permitted for me to do so." *What did I just say? No! I take it back!*

"Good! It is settled then!

Chapter 4: Yeshua The Messiah

We arrived and were greeted with much fanfare. Josiah's brother greeted us with a loud and boisterous laugh. *Yep, this is definitely Josiah's brother!* He was not too unlike his sibling. He was a large man, but not as much width around the middle. He apparently wasn't as fond of food as Josiah was. He was younger, and not as calloused as his big brother. It was very evident that he had things a lot easier. Simon filled me in on the family history while we made our way to Cana. His uncle Haran married into money. His wife Norah became the only child when her older brother died at a young age. It's said that at least five other brothers were stillborn. With no son to inherit the land, it fell to her husband when they married.

Cana was typically a great producer of wine in the region. The environment made it very profitable for those who worked the land here. However, Haran's crops were damaged by a couple of years of drought and were unable to supply the wine for his son's wedding. This is where Josiah's wine from Korazim comes into play. They have had bountiful crops, and business has been good.

"Well, well Simon… I am pleased to see you! Is my wine on its way?" Haran wasted no time in getting down to business.

"Yes Uncle, we brought some from Tiberias to start out the celebration, and the wine from Korazim will be here in a few more days."

"Your father has told me that you have a head for business. Are you enjoying the responsibilities that he has entrusted to you?"

"Yes Uncle, I do... very much!"

"Well, we will see how well you do. I expect a favorable price for your loving uncle, eh Simon?"

"It will be as fair as it can be for such a good crop last year. This wine is made from the biggest, juiciest grapes I have seen in a long while. The wine is now at its best!"

"Simon... be gentle. I am family, remember?" They both laughed as Simon motioned for me to come over.

"Uncle, this is my friend Benjamin. He will be helping us this week." I waited for a bear hug, but instead Haran greeted me with the customary kiss on both cheeks.

"Benjamin, would you excuse us? We have details to go over. My son Nathaniel will help you get settled in." Haran waved his son over. He and Simon walked away as Nathaniel approached me.

"Greetings! I am Nathaniel, you must be Benjamin."

"Yes, I am... how did you know?" He looked over his shoulder. I followed his gaze to the cart that Leah and Samuel were on.

"Samuel speaks well of you... you did a good thing; taking care of his leg like that... very interesting. I have never seen anything like it."

"Yes, and Samuel is also drunk!" Nathaniel and I both laughed in unison.

"True, but Leah is not." I had no desire to explain myself again. "No matter... come with me to the house." As we walked, Nathaniel started sharing something that astounded me.

"I am very excited about the wedding feast; we will have a very special guest with us! Have you heard of Yeshua of Nazareth?" My heart stopped... *Yeshua? Wedding at Cana?* Now I know the time period I am in! Yeshua turned the water into wine about 30 A.D. There has been a lot of speculation as to whether any miracles really happened during the time of the Prophet's ministry or not. Obviously, knowing what I know now, we run out of wine... then the better wine from Korazim shows up and it may have been perceived as a miracle. As I considered my deductive reasoning, Nathaniel continued.

"I know what you are thinking Benjamin." *If you only knew!* "Can anything good come out of Nazareth? You know... these were my exact words when my friend Philip of Bethesda told me about Him. As I walked toward this man, He spoke to me as if he knew me. Then He told me about standing under a fig tree... He said he *saw* me! Before Philip even asked me to go with him! This man is the Son of God! He has to be! He is the man spoken of by the prophets!" He beamed with excitement, and I too was excited to meet such a historical and well-known figure.

The rest of the day was hurried, but when the sun began to set, everything went quiet. I hadn't practiced the Jewish Sabbath in many years. Sunday was *my* Sabbath... with sports, chips, and beer; which were my religion of choice. My wife would take our children to church and I would stay home and watch the game. It never bothered me that our children weren't raised in the Jewish Faith. It had been dead to me a long time. I felt that as long as they were getting some form or fashion of a religion, they would turn out fine. I missed my family.

I woke up to the sound of screaming. It was dark, but there was a fire . . . and rain . . . and . . .

"Ben! Ben... help us!" It was Sarah. I scrambled to my feet and ran to the vehicle. It was demolished and Sarah and the children were trapped inside. The fire was beginning spread to the front seat of the SUV. Sarah began to scream.

"Oh my God! Ben – we can't get out! Help us!" Emily and Jacob were in the back, pounding on the windows.

"Daddy! It hurts! Please! Get us out of here!" I stood watching as the flames converged on my family. I was frozen... I couldn't move. Suddenly, their expressions changed... their faces contorted. Their skin began to char from the fire as they bared their teeth and shouted at me in a frightful, wicked way.

"You did this! You killed us!" All three of them let out a scream of horror that turned into a guttural, evil laughter. They somehow leapt out of the vehicle and charged at me with demonic faces, and gruesome, hideous bodies.

In an instant, they were on me... cutting at my clothes with their razor-like black talons and gnashing at me with their lurid teeth. Two of them pinned me to the ground as one stood over me with its claws on my chest. Bulging eyes... black... dark, so evil. Its throat gurgled and popped as it breathed in and out. Then it spoke to me.

"Daddy . . . why Daddy?" Its voice was like Emily's – so soft and sweet. "Daddy . . . why did you let me *DIE*?" The soft, gentle voice turned into a roar that pierced me with a fear I had never known before. The demon bent over me. It's hot, sulfurous breath stinging my face and its claws digging deep into my chest. The pain was immense! I screamed in horror!

I sat up in bed; sweat was dripping off of me like I'd just gotten out of the shower. I was soaked! My heart felt as if it would explode out of my chest, and my breath was labored. *It was a nightmare... just a nightmare.*

I looked around. Simon and the others were already gone. I tried to get up, but I was having difficulty; I was shaking so badly. I brought my hands up to my chest in an effort to calm my heart. I felt something wet and slippery. I looked at my hands and chest. There was blood everywhere. *Whaaa?* I looked closer at my chest and saw that there were ten, distinct puncture wounds... five on each side of my chest. I have heard of dreams being manifested into reality before; people dreaming of burning their hand and waking up to find they were really hurt. There were numerous stories, but I passed them off as urban legends. This, however, was very real... and very painful!

I made my way to the water basin and moistened a towel. I poured some wine on it and began cleaning my wounds. *So strange...* I patted the cloth on my chest. The fog in my brain lifted and I began to remember my dream in more detail. My family's faces... their screams... their accusations. My knees buckled and my legs gave way. I found myself on my knees with my hands still on the table... grasping for support. My nails dug into the wood, anchoring me. Preparing me for the dam that was about to break.

Their faces... they wouldn't leave my thoughts. They stayed there, etched in my mind... begging me. My chest began to heave as the sobbing began; first, in silent tremors, then tears began to fall like water dripping from the trees after a hard rain. I fought for breath, seeming to find none; then it came... a wave of release. Relentless wave after wave of soul wrenching cries from the deep places of my heart. Pain had been kept prisoner there for so long, that cries of anguish escaped my lips when it found its way to the surface.

"I'm so sorry... I'm sorry I failed you."

The picture of them began to transform from one of agony to one of peace. I saw my family as I had known them so often... smiling, and happy. They would never condemn me for what happened. Knowing this, how could I have held such contempt for myself for so long?

Sarah would nag me about going to their church, or being more involved with Emily's recitals and Jake's football games. But more often than not, she was so loving and forgiving, especially after she became a Believer. To Emily... my sweet young lady, I was a man who could do no wrong in her eyes... and Jacob? We were best buds. I was his hero. No... they would never condemn me. It wasn't my fault. I sighed, and then spoke out loud."

"It wasn't my fault."

I got to my feet feeling fifty pounds lighter. Immediately, I looked around the room to make sure no one had come in while I was having my little "episode". All was quiet. I walked to the window and looked out. The sun was already up, casting its long, stark shadows on the land. This time, instead of an orchard view, I had one of the livestock. The smell that accompanied it was not reminiscent of a blossoming orchard either. In spite of its stench, I felt as if nothing could spoil this beautiful day. I was finally free of the hell I was living in, and now could live life to the fullest.

Simon entered the room and immediately gasped after seeing the bloody puncture wounds on my chest.

"Are you alright? Benjamin, what happened to you?" I looked down at my chest again. The bleeding had stopped, but I had not finished cleaning up.

"It's not as bad as it looks." I turned back to the table and resumed cleaning my wounds. Simon walked up beside me, pulled on my shoulder to turn and face him. He asked again.

"What happened?" He closely examined the wounds and spoke in an agitated whisper. "Who did this to you? Were you sleeping when this happened? Did you see them? I will find out who did this and have them stoned!" He was showing such anger now. This was a side of him I had not yet seen.

"Yes, I was asleep, but no one came in the room and did this to me." Simon cocked his head to the side and questioned me with his eyes. I continued. "I was dreaming about my family. They were on fire, but I couldn't help them. They started accusing me of killing them... then their appearance changed. They turned into demons and attacked me." Simon stepped back.

"Demons did this to you? These spirits are troubling you... why?

"I believe it was to keep me bound. For a long time, I have allowed them to trouble my mind and my thoughts. They were casting blame on me for the deaths of my family... but now I am free! I carry no burden now! It wasn't my fault!" Simon's eyes welled up with tears as he joined me in my celebration.

"He will answer!"

"And he will hear!" We laughed together until we could no longer.

Joy was something vacant in my life. What a relief to have found it again.

"We will go now to the Synagogue. The reading of the Scriptures will testify to your freedom. Come... we will give much thanks!"

The Synagogue was located in the middle of Cana. It was a beautiful piece of architecture. To see these buildings in a new state and not a pile of rubble or in great need of repair, was refreshing. Once inside... I was even more amazed! It was breathtaking! The main floor, which was reserved for the men, was vast and open.

There were pillars running down either side of the hall providing support for the second floor, which was open as well. Banisters ran the full length, offering a view from the women's gallery. In the center, three quarters to the back of the Synagogue, was a stone table in which the scrolls were laid out and read. Behind that, the seat of Moses, where the Synagogue ruler sat. On the back wall was the Cabinet where the Torah was kept; the modern day Ark of the Synagogue. It had the shape of a small house. It was about two feet deep and had a pitched roof that fell to the sides. It had a cabinet-like door that swung open to reveal eight sections – all containing the different scrolls making up the Torah. People were still filing in when Haran walked up to us.

"Simon told me you are a Rabbi and would like to read from the Scrolls this morning... we would be honored to have you do so."

No sense in explaining that I wasn't really a Rabbi. Haran was obviously a lay official, or on the Council of Elders. He seemed to be directing the goings on here. Soon all were in their places. Knowing that I was about to read to those standing before me put butterflies in my stomach.

I remembered the first time I gave a Lecture. I was petrified, thinking that the students would be laughing and joking about me as they left the auditorium. I spent the better half of the two weeks prior, fretting about it; Sarah let me in on a little secret that could help curb my anxiety.

"In my speech class, I was always terrified to be speaking in front of so many people, so I began picking out a friendly face in the crowd... and spoke to that one person. It made it so much easier for me. I even got an A in that class!" She beamed... I, on the other hand, remembered the difficulty in my speech classes. I passed with a C-.

"Rabbi... Rabbi? You will begin." Haran took his seat and I took my place at the beautiful stone lectern. I reached into the far corners of my memories and managed to pull up a list of procedures for ancient Synagogue worship. The Shema' is out of Deuteronomy chapter 6. I cleared my throat, and began the Shema'...

> "*Sh'ma Yisra'eil Adonai Eloheinu, Adonai echad.*
> *Barukh sheim k'vod malkhuto l'olam va'ed.*
> *V'ahav'ta eit Adonai Elohekha b'khol l'vav'kha uv'khol naf'sh'kha uv'khol m'odekha.*
> *V'hayu had'varim ha'eileh asher anokhi m'tzav'kha hayom al l'vavekha.*
> *V'shinan'tam l'vanekha v'dibar'ta bam b'shiv't'kha b'veitekha uv'lekh't'kha vaderekh uv'shakh'b'kha uv'kumekha*
> *Uk'shar'tam l'ot al yadekha v'hayu l'totafot bein einekha.*
> *Ukh'tav'tam al m'zuzot beitekha uvish'arekha.*
> (In English, the Shema' is as follows...)

"Hear O Israel: The Lord our God, the Lord is one! Blessed be the Name of His glorious kingdom for ever and ever. You shall love the Lord your God with all your heart, with all your soul, and with all your strength. And these words that I command you today shall be in your heart. And you shall teach them diligently to your children, and you shall speak of them when you sit at home, and when you walk along the way, and when you lie down and when you rise

up. And you shall bind them as a sign on your hand, and they shall be for frontlets between your eyes. And you shall write them on the doorposts of your house and on your gates."

My nerves bristled to the surface again, so I looked for that one kind face in the crowd. In the back… midway on the left, I saw him. *Now this was a kind face.* My fears subsided as I read from the Law and the Prophets. Each scripture seamlessly flowed like poetry from my lips. I became more relaxed and confident by the minute as I continued to look into the man's eyes. After the prayer, I looked up and he was gone. *I wanted to meet him. Why did he leave?*

Thanksgiving and exhortations finished out the service.

"Well done Benjamin!" Haran and Simon both said almost in unison. Simon continued.

"I told you Uncle, that he would bring something fresh and exciting. Benjamin, you spoke with such conviction and passion! Wonderful! Wonderful!"

I was pleased to be functioning as a normal human being again, let alone, back in a Synagogue and acting in the calling I first had as a boy… it was surreal.

"Thank you so much for allowing me to be a part of your worship today… I am honored. By the way, do you know the man who was sitting on the left side, near the back, that left during prayer? Did you see him leave?" Haran and Simon looked confused. Haran was the first to speak.

"No one left – it would be disruptive to the worship. It is not allowed!" I described in detail, as best I could, the man I saw. "No such man" Haran replied. "I saw no man like that here. I am familiar with every man, woman, and child that attend our Synagogue and know most of them quite well. I tell you… I saw no such man."

"I as well." Simon interjected. "You have had an interesting morning!" I caught his meaning by the look in his eyes. I had a very traumatic experience, and it could be that I was imagining it. "None the less... you did well my friend!" He embraced me then led me over to a young man that seemed to be the center of attention in the small group.

"Benjamin, this is Amir. He is the one who is in celebration to be married." Amir was beaming from ear to ear as his peers chimed in agreement and slapped him on the back. "Amir, Benjamin will be helping us with this week's festivities." Amir took my hand in greeting.

"Your reading was inspiring! Much more exciting than the drudgery we are used to hearing." Haran overheard his comment and shot him a glare. He backed down on his enthusiasm. He placed a fist over his mouth and cleared his throat. "It was *good.*"

"So... you are the fortunate one, eh?" I said. His friends started laughing and giving him the preverbal "ball and chain" expletives, in ancient Israeli terminology, of course.

"I *AM* fortunate!" He playfully rebuked his friends with his stare and continued. "My wife . . . er . . . betrothed is over there." He pointed her out with a smile on his face. "Her name is Atarah. We are pleased to have you attending our wedding Rabbi". With that, his friends drug him away. He looked back apologetically, and waved goodbye

"See there Benjamin!" Simon was beaming like a kid showing off a new toy. "You have a gift."

The rest of the day was perfect for recharging. In spite of my sore chest, I managed a time of rest and prayer. What was God trying to tell me in this experience? I felt renewed, and I wanted to be of value again. I still caught myself fighting with the past...

like *I don't deserve to teach the Word of God and lead a service in a Synagogue. Who do I think I am?* I had experienced victory this morning only to fight in another battle this afternoon.

As I finished praying, I felt such a stinging pain in my chest. It felt like a thousand needles poking me! I opened my garment and saw that the sores were getting infected... they were oozing puss. *I cleaned it well. I should not be experiencing any infection so soon.* I re-cleaned the wound and found it very tender to the touch. I decided that instead of letting it breathe, I better dress the wound. I did what was needed and took off in search of Simon.

The sun had gone down... the Sabbath was over; and preparations had begun for the wedding feast. I could smell the baking of bread and other delicacies. Oh, what a heavenly smell! I then realized how ravished I was. I felt as if I hadn't eaten in days. As a matter of fact, it had been four days! No wonder I was so hungry. I was very thankful to have my appetite back.

I followed my nose and found the bakers hard at work; but more than willing to fulfill my need for food. My stomach was soon full, but something was missing inside. I felt fulfilled and free... yet just on the edge of it. I had arrived at my destination but couldn't seem to step across into the promise land, so to speak. I wrestled with my emotions and found it an exhausting endeavor. I wasn't winning, so I called it a night and slept without dreaming at all.

Chapter 5: The Wedding Feast

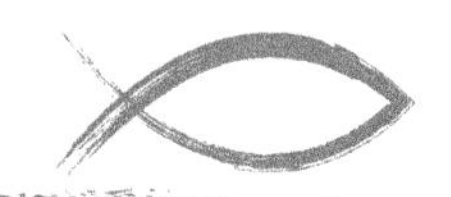

The next few days were spent eating, drinking, dancing – and more eating. It was definitely a joyous occasion… I was even having fun! Soon, I found myself seeking out our important guest that was supposed to come. To my knowledge, Yeshua wasn't here. Things were going well until Simon received word from his servant that the wine from Korazim hadn't arrived yet. The wine was already running low and the festivities showed no sign of slowing. Simon was in a panic.

"No, this cannot be…Who told you of this?" The servant bowed, and then shared in detail, again what he knew.

"Master, I received word, just moments ago, from Ethan. He and two others escaped with their lives! Thieves attacked, killing the rest, but these three were spared. They were bound, and then they watched as these horrible men stole the wine and other supplies from Korazim. They worked free of their restraints and made haste here as fast as they could run. It's all gone Master! Forgive them for their folly…they failed you."

"No Melech. Tell them they are not responsible for this. Make sure they are well cared for."

"But Master, Haran will be fierce with anger! He will be held responsible for this. The bride's father will find *him* at fault! What shall we do?"

"How much wine is left?"

"Only enough to last until evening."

"Leave us, and attend to the other servants. There must be a way. I need time to think." Simon was distraught. In these times, something like this had the potential of great embarrassment. The groom's family could be sued, and the wedding called off. Simon would be held responsible for this.

"Haran will disown me Benjamin! Not just him...but my father as well! He will be furious! He entrusted this to me! I should have thought to have more servants guarding the shipment. There have been many reports of these robberies and attacks lately...but I thought it wouldn't happen to us. How foolish!" I tried my best to comfort my friend, but to no avail. Simon left me to pursue a solution to the wine shortage, and I turned toward the crowd and began my search for the man I saw at the Synagogue. Maybe he's here. Nathaniel nearly ran over me as he made his way through the crowd. Just as I looked up, I was able to prevent the collision. I threw up my hands and cushioned the blow. Nathaniel turned to face me.

"He's here! The Son of God...The King of Israel...He is here!" He was bursting with excitement. "Come with me!"

"Oww!" Nathaniel grabbed my upper arm, pulling me through the masses. "Take care of my arm Nathaniel...you'll tear it off!" He only looked back and smiled.

"Hurry! You must meet Him! He is here with my friends and His mother. Quickly Benjamin!"

"I am...I am...just don't break my arm!"

As we approached them, I realized that *Yeshua* was *the man* from the Synagogue. The one I picked out in the crowd to look at! The same eyes...same calm expression. Our eyes met and when he recognized me, He smiled. Nathaniel came to a screeching halt before the crowd of people.

"Andrew, Phillip, Peter, John.... my friends, this is my friend Benjamin. Benjamin, I'd also like you to meet Yeshua, and His mother Mary. Welcome Mother.... Yeshua. We are honored to have you here!" Mary spoke first,

"Thank you, Nathaniel, you know we wouldn't miss this!"

Yeshua still had not spoken. For thousands of years, we have tried to picture Moses, Abraham, David and many other great men of God. Artists have made renditions on canvas in an attempt to personify these men. Others have tried to capture the essence of them by carving them out of stone. Now I stand before a great prophet... waiting to hear his voice. Will it echo like thunder? Will he speak and cause me to fall to my death? Will his voice be still and quiet? The man standing before me definitely did not *look* like the blue-eyed Jesus depicted in paintings found popular among the Church. In fact, Sarah had a picture of Yeshua in the hallway of our home... knocking on a door. This is not him! This man looked.... well, normal. Short dark hair...beard... Jewish looking. If it weren't for the knowledge of who stood before me, I could pass him on the street and not look twice. However, there *was* something about him; just like in the Synagogue. One look in his kind eyes, and all fear subsided. A little unnerving was the fact that it felt as though he saw me.... to the real me. The one no one else has ever known. I began to feel very uncomfortable, so I looked away. Yeshua spoke directly to me.

"Benjamin, why do you fear? Has God not brought you here to fulfill your destiny? Has He not provided the way for you? Listen to me. I am who you seek, but many trials you will have to endure to follow me."

Does He know? Who I am? Where I come from? I was aghast. What do I say to that? I felt as though He was reading my mail.... I didn't like it at all! God had done many things in me so far, but now Yeshua was speaking of *trials* and *enduring*. This was too much to take in right now.

"Please excuse me." I left the situation as quickly as I could, leaving Nathaniel to apologize for my rudeness. This Yeshua was different! I'd never felt so intimidated in someone's presence before, yet so comforted. *What is going on?*

I found Simon and got busy helping him ration the wine. He groaned with misery while he mulled over the predicament in his head.

"What am I going to do?" He whispered to himself. I took my opportunity to speak. I knew what could be done.

"Simon, Yeshua of Nazareth is here." His attention was weak.

"He is? My whole life is over! Arrgh!

"I think you should talk to Yeshua... or his mother. See if they can help in any way." He thought for a moment, and then a light seemed to come on.

"Should I bother them with this? Nathaniel speaks all the time about this man and how great he is. I am at my end. What else can I do?"

Did I just write history? Simon dropped what he was doing and immediately took some servants with him and sought out this last hope. I didn't want to miss this! I followed close behind; distancing myself a little so as not to come in close proximity of Yeshua again. I was so drawn to him, yet so afraid. Simon found Mary and began explaining the situation. Mary nodded to him, then went over and spoke with her Son.

"Yeshua, my Son, they are out of wine." Yeshua looked at her and said.

"Woman, what is it that you expect me to do? It is not yet my time." Mary summoned us.

"Whatever he wants you to do... do it." Yeshua stood and walked over to the servants and me.

"Fill the water pots over there with water." He was talking about six stone jars that were set aside for purification rights, or ceremonial washing. Without hesitation, they began hauling water to the stone jars. Each one was big... holding about thirty gallons apiece. When they were done, he turned to me. "Draw from the jar and take it to the Master of the Feast."

Me? This was too much! I stepped up to the vessels of water and picked up a cup. Dipping it into the jar... seeing only water, I drew it out to find a deep red wine! To make sure, I looked in all six stone jars and found them *all* full of wine! I was amazed! I did as Yeshua said and took the cup to the bride's father and presented him with it. He drank... stopped... and looked at me; and with his brow raised in question, he took another drink. He stood up and shouted.

"Everyone usually uses up the good wine at the beginning of the feast, then waters it down as the days come to an end. But here... Amir saves the best wine for now! I am blessed and honored!" He raised his cup. "To Amir and his house!" The guests burst into applause. Simon was next to Haran as the announcement was made. When it was finished, he pulled Simon to him, slapping him on the back with delight. "You have done very well Simon! I think you will find an extra gold shekel in your payment! You have in turn, brought honor to my household! Thank you, Nephew!"

Simon was speechless. The last information he had was that the stone jars were filled with water. He was about to share his concern with Haran just as the announcement was made. He looked toward Yeshua and then combed the crowd… searching. He saw me, broke free of his uncle and made a b-line for me. The look on his face was bewilderment.

"Tell me it's true! We have wine… but how?" I couldn't wait to tell the story.

"I wouldn't have believed it myself if I hadn't been the one to actually draw the wine from the jar. It was water… I dipped the cup in and drew out wine! Right before my eyes, Simon! I saw it!

"Who is this Yeshua? I am told that he is from Nazareth. Of all things… of all places. The city is nothing… yet such marvels come from its bosom?" He stared off into space, trying to compute what just happened. I left his side, as he muttered to himself, without him even noticing. I wanted to find Yeshua this time, and talk to him.

Some of the disciples had scattered among the people. Mary was speaking with the bride to be. *Where are you?* I was scanning the guests when I caught a glimpse of Him sitting at the edge of the courtyard on a small stone fence. I was intrigued by Him. *Why?* I fought through the rowdy crowd and sat down beside Him… and questioned Him.

"May I sit with you?" He seemed deep in thought as he searched the ground for something. Without breaking His gaze, He responded.

"Benjamin, did you know that every grain of sand and every rock is unique? None are alike." He paused for a moment. "Such love and care was put into our Fathers creation. Everything has a purpose… perfectly balanced for our use and enjoyment. We break the ground with our plow, and it provides nourishment and protection for the seed to grow. We use stone to build… this fence, or a great temple." *I wish I knew what he was getting at. I wanted to know more about my destiny… not rocks!*

"Yeshua, you said before that I was here to fulfill my destiny? What did you mean by that?

"Do you believe?"

"Believe what?" *I'm getting tired of these riddles!*

"Benjamin, I ask you these questions in order to make you think..." *Whaaa? Is he reading my mind, or what?* He reached down and picked up a rock "He created you." With this statement... my heart of stone began to crack and chip off a little. "Benjamin, you have a destiny to fulfill as much as this dirt..." He moved the dirt around with his foot. "...and this rock..." Holding the rock in the palm of his hand, he continued. "This dirt... and this rock, were created for a purpose. Just as the ground needs to be broken up in order to plant, and rocks must be hewn and put in place in order to build; so must *your* life be shaped and molded for the perfection of our Fathers work in you. You... in and of yourself, cannot determine your own purpose. It is by God's hand..." He held up the rock for me to see again, and then threw it into the field. "... that we are able to *move* in *His* purpose and for His Kingdom." My mind was coming up short on his reasoning. *What has my life got to do with all of this?*

"What has my life got to do with all of this Yeshua?"

"In time, you will know. Your heart is searching for answers. Follow it... follow me and you will find what you are looking for. When the wedding is over, I will be going to Capernaum. You are welcome to come along."

"I will speak with Simon. Maybe he will come too." Yeshua smiled as he stood up.

"Perhaps he will. Now... let's celebrate with the others, shall we?"

I didn't quite understand all that Yeshua spoke about, but I had a feeling I would soon enough. We walked over to where Nathaniel and his friends were busy discussing the wondrous miracle that took place tonight. I got some more wine and began to drink. The taste of this wine was unexpected. It had to be the best wine I have ever tasted! To think it came from the water in six stone jars. What manner of man is this? I have to find out.

Chapter 6: Matters of the Heart

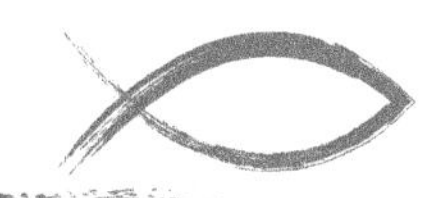

The wedding was beautiful. It made me sad to think what Sarah and I missed out on. We were married by His Honor, George G. Gumbolt, in Altoona Pennsylvania. Our wedding was heartfelt, but not much for memories, except the laughter we shared concerning the size of the diamond in her wedding band.

Amir and Atarah were off to a great start in life… and *we* were off to Tiberias. I spoke in detail about my conversation with Yeshua, and Simon shared my enthusiasm in following him to Capernaum. We speculated as to what kind of miracle would come next.

"Do you think he is the actual Son of God?" Simon threw out the question after a few moments of silence. "This man has truly done something miraculous… but… the Son of God?"

"I know… my mind is confused as well. The Prophets spoke of one such as him. Only time will tell. That's why I want to follow him and see for myself."

There was no denying that Yeshua was special. He had something about him that just seemed... well… right. He looked like an ordinary man, but power, authority, and love flowed from him!

"Whew! Benjamin, we must rest." Simon shuffled over to some large rocks and sat on one of them. "Here… sit." He patted the rock next to him and I sat down. We both just stared at the caravan of weary people as they went slowly by. "Do you think he has come to free our people from the oppression of the Romans? Is he going to build an army to rise up against them?" I of course knew the answer to that one.

"I don't think so Simon, but I think he will stir things up a bit. His words seem to be that of love, not uprising or war."

"Hey Benjamin... Simon!" Samuel waved from the cart as it passed by. "I'm going to get home first!" He moved a little with excitement, then winced from pain and grabbed his leg.

"It will be hard to keep him down." Simon said as he pulled the cork on the wineskin. He took a drink, and then held it out to me. "Wine?"

"Yes... thank you." My mouth was so parched; it felt as if my tongue was cracked open like the arid ground of the Mojave Desert. The wine from the wedding feast was so invigorating. Immediately, the thirst was gone, and I felt refreshed. "Have you ever had such wine?"

"No... never. It seems to quench my thirst better and bring new life to my weary bones. In fact, I am ready to continue." He stood up and started walking, then realized I wasn't following. "Are you coming?"

"No... I think I will sit awhile longer. You go on. I will catch up." Simon shrugged and continued on without me. I guess the wine got me thinking. *Could this really be the Son of God?*

Sarah was busy putting the canned goods away while I finished up with the wine and refrigerated items.

"So... You still haven't answered me yet, honey." I was trying to avoid this at all cost.

"Really? I thought I already gave you an answer." I was lying... *Better fess up, Ben* "Aw Sarah... you know how I feel about your church. I know it's been good for you and the children, but I don't think it's for me. I'm Jewish, remember?" There was a hint of a snicker mixed with my words, but Sarah found no humor in it.

"You told Jacob you would be there for his baptism! You promised him! Do you know how excited he is about you coming? It would mean the world to him... to all of us!" The package of frozen peas began to numb my hand as I stood there contemplating my dilemma.

"I'll go... for Jake." She gave me the puppy dog look. "And for you and Emily." I turned around to face the refrigerator again. "But don't think this is going to be a regular thing!" Sarah came up and snuggled in behind and wrapped her arms around me. I threw the peas in the freezer and shut the door. "You know I love you... right?" She moved around to face me.

"Yes, I know that Ben... and I love you. That's why I won't give up on you so easily. I know you hold some very deep scars from what your father did to you. I just want you to be free of the hurt, and only Jesus can do that for you."

"I don't hurt!" I had a habit of lying to myself, and to her about this.

"Ben... from the moment you left home, you have been out to prove something. My goodness, the class load you took on at college would have killed anyone else! I hardly saw you unless I spent time with you in the library. And don't forget that our honeymoon was cut short because you 'had to get your dissertation done' ahead of schedule. You have been working with a fire lit under your 'you know what' for about twelve years now. You stay busy so you won't have to deal with the feelings concerning your father."

She cut right through me… like a floodlight examining my soul and all of its dark and dirty places… my private places.

"You amaze me Ben. I don't know how you can juggle family, work, and more school like you do. One of these days, the dam is going to break, and Jesus will be the only one who can pick up the pieces and keep you from drowning. Remember this sweetheart… what you do has an impact on our family… not just on you. We hurt with you, and as long as you hold on to that pain and anger, it eats away at the fiber of our family."

She kissed me softly and looked long and hard in my eyes. For a moment there, I felt something happening. My heart was giving way. Letting go of control scared me to death, and panic went off in my head like a three-alarm fire. My exterior shell was crumbling… but like a flash, the walls went up again and I was safe. Sarah smiled once more at me and then went about putting the grocery bags away. I was ready to play the role in church tonight.

"Hello again!" I looked up from my dirty feet and found a big, smelly, hairy man standing in front of me.

"Peter… is it?"

"Yes... from the wedding. Where is the rest of your clan? Are you traveling alone?" As he finished speaking, Phillip, Andrew, and Nathaniel walked up, followed by John and Yeshua.

"Greetings… Benjamin!" Nathaniel hailed. "Yeshua said you will be joining us in Capernaum. I am so glad you are coming! You will not be disappointed! You must walk with us… come!" Nathaniel came over and pulled me to my feet. Yeshua smiled.

"Good to see you Ben... I was expecting you." *There he goes again!* "Walk with me." The rest of the men took the hint and went on ahead, laughing and talking.

"Quite a coincidence meeting up with you like this." I started the conversation... I was nervous.

"You believe this was a coincidence, Benjamin?" Somehow, I knew it wasn't.

"I... uh... don't know. Maybe not." He smiled and we walked in silence for a while. I couldn't help but study him. *The Son of God. This man is the Son of God?*

"Do you have questions Benjamin? Why do you think you are here?" There was silence. He very effectively left me hanging and would not continue speaking until I had answered him. I thought for a moment.

"Is it because I have been blaming myself for my family's death? If that's what it is... then I have experienced freedom from that! A great miracle was done in my life yesterday! I no longer blame myself – my heart is healed!"

"Is it? Look and see. Look at your heart." He seemed to mean it literally, so I did it. I opened my garment. It pulled at the wounds on my chest. They broke open again... oozing puss. It looked as though the sores were bigger... more open. *Whew!* The stench!

"Yeshua, I don't understand. This happened to me in a dream. Still, I think this was very real. Was it?"

"Real in the sense that it was a spiritual attack? Yes, it manifested itself in the physical. You see, the outward appearance cannot always hide the actions or will of the heart. Know this, Benjamin, the heart is wicked and deceitful above all else! Without God, you are of *this* World. You are under the influence of Satan. Apart from the Father, no good is found in anyone . . . only evil."

"But Yeshua, I *AM* good... more so now than ever before! I want to be a Rabbi again! How can I be under the influence of Satan?"

From some dark place inside, anger was teeming up in me. I was insulted. I know the scripture like the back of my hand. *My* intentions were honorable, and *He* is telling me I'm evil?

"I was beginning to think You *were* the Son of God! But now I see that You are no different than all the rest of the Christians I've met." Bitterness began to boil in me. "You all speak of love, but expect me to change *my* life, and *my* views. You speak of happiness. Where did that get my family? They served You... now they're DEAD!"

I couldn't take it any longer. I ran as far, and as fast away from Him as my feet could carry me. Tears were streaming down my dusty face, leaving a trail of mud on my cheeks. I ran until my lungs were hurting. Finally... I had to stop. I could see Simon's caravan in the distance now, but I hadn't the strength nor desire to catch up with them. I sat right down in the middle of the road and wept.

"Why... why did you take them from me?"

I gritted my teeth and swore to never cry again. My breath quickened, and I could feel my heart racing. My mind was getting foggy, and my anger was becoming clear. *This... this is how I survive. This is my comfort.* I could hear laughing. A strange but familiar feeling overtook me. Horrible thoughts filled my mind, and comforting voices prodded me. *Yes... it wasn't your fault. It was HIS fault! God took them from you!*

Chapter 7: Demons Flee

Dusk was upon me as I came to one of the watchtowers of Josiah's orchard. I welcomed the night... it was comforting.

"Simon will question you... what will you say?" I turned to see who was whispering to me, only to find no one there.

"Yesssss... what will you say... what will you do?"

I was disappointed in Simon. *He's just like the other's... he wants to follow HIM!*

"Don't trust him... don't trust anyone!"

I don't trust him. I walked up the road to the house. The light illuminating from it was somehow thwarting. *Can I go in?* Someone startled me from the darkness.

"Benjamin? Is that you?" The man walked closer and appeared in the dim light. "It's me... Gehazi! We have been worried about you. I saw you from the watchtower. I was waiting for you. Simon will be relieved you are here... come!" I backed slowly away as if cornered... hesitant. "Are you well? What's wrong?"

"Lie to him! Don't tell him about us!"

"You must go in... we have work to do!"

"Yesss... we have much work to do!"

I stammered a little then gained my composure somehow.

"I guess I am weary from travel." I stepped forward and walked with him to the house. There was little activity going on except for a small group of men, apparently having a meeting of sorts. Simon looked up and grinned.

"Ben! You are here! I have... uh... *WE* have been worried about you! I didn't expect you would be along so far behind us. Glad you are here... come and sit with us. We are discussing what to do. We have been sharing with Menehem here. He wants to come with us to see Yeshua!" *Oww!* A searing pain shot through me. It seemed as if a thousand screams went off in my head.

"Ssssstop! Stop it! Don't say that name!"

"HIM?" I screamed. He is not the Son of God! Don't waste any time seeking after HIM! He is just a man like you and me... but filled with trickery and deceit!" My hatred of this man had grown ten-fold! I felt so out of control. *What is happening to me?* "I spent some time with this Ye... this man. I can assure you He is no Messiah!"

"Yes... Yes!"

"Go on... Go on!"

"I overheard his disciples talking about how they fooled everyone and how you... you Simon..." I pointed at him and bared my teeth. "...gave Him a gold shekel because you felt He was more deserving than you! FOOL! You have been had!" They stared at me with disbelief and sank back down in their seats. "Three month's wages Simon... You know how many people in need could have used that money? You gave it to a false prophet! We were all fooled... especially me!"

"It's working... look at them!"

"Yes... go on! He took your wife!"

"He took your children! Ha!"

"Benjamin, what has happened to you? You are not yourself!"

"No! This IS me!"

The laughter... and the screams were deafening! *Stop it! Please stop it!* I put my hands over my ears and tried to stifle the noise, but it seemed to make it worse. I staggered and lost my balance. Simon and Josiah came to me... grabbing each one of my arms to support me.

"The pain... The anger! Make it stop Simon!"

Blood started wicking into my tunic. My chest area was soaked. It was pouring out of the infected puncture wounds. I buckled and sank to the floor. Josiah and Simon could not hold me up. I fell back, lying on the floor looking up at *them* again. *They* had me pinned.

"Yesss... the poison is in you!"

"Give in to us! Give in to the Prince of Darkness!"

"You are ours! Yes... you belong to us now!"

Incessant laughter was all I could hear or see. It was a spirit-world of evil. All I could feel was life spilling from my body. A pool of blood was forming beneath me. The pressure on my chest made it impossible to breathe. I was in a panic and fading fast when a light shown all around me... dim at first. The demons stepped back with fear in their bulbous eyes. *Yeshua... Please help me...*

"SPIRITS COME OUT!"

Something like the sound of a clap of thunder vibrated the whole building. The vision of a man in blinding white garments and fire in His eyes was chasing them away. *Gone... they're gone now.*

"He's waking up!" I heard someone say. I opened my eyes, but everything was out of focus. I saw what looked like faces staring down at me. I started thrashing about in fear, thinking *they* had come back for me.

"They're back! Get away! Yeshua... Help me!"

"I am here Benjamin, don't be afraid. I am here."

I rubbed my eyes and opened them again. Things came into focus. I could see faces now. They weren't demons. They were Simon, Gehazi, Josiah… and Yeshua. The moment I looked in His eyes… I broke.

"Yeshua… please forgive me, I am so ashamed! I said some horrible things about You!" I began sobbing.

"Child, you are forgiven." He put his hand on my head and all fear left me. A wonderful peace came over me.

"Yeshua… why was I tormented so?"

"Because your bitterness… and anger towards God opened a door for the Enemy to enter. Satan seeks to destroy you, but I have come to give you life and victory in my name. Stay pure before God and seek after Him with all your heart. If you do this… they cannot return."

"Why didn't I do this when Sarah wanted me to? Maybe they'd still be alive?"

"Ben… guard your heart. It is not good to dwell on the past. Think on the *good* things of God and know that *He* has a plan for you. What Satan had intended for evil… Our Father has purposed it for good!"

Simon questioned Yeshua. "How can the loss of his wife and children be a *good* thing? It has all but destroyed him?" Yeshua turned and looked at me. He allowed me to answer.

"I think I know now. Finally, it is clear to me. My family knew God and I didn't. They spent years trying to turn my heart toward Him… and probably would have continued to try for many more years to come. I would not have turned. I was too selfish and hard-hearted. I was too wrapped up in my own little world to want to be a part of theirs. The horrible loss of my family has brought me to where I am now. It has not been easy…" I looked at Yeshua. "… but what I have found has taken away the pain. My family is in a very good place."

This revelation made it hard to contain my excitement. I was ready to start ministering. I had the head knowledge… now I have the heart.

"Yeshua, I am ready to begin ministry… when can I start?" He smiled at me and graciously asked if we could be left alone.

"Goodnight Benjamin. Peaceful sleep." Josiah turned and left the room. Simon remained standing there.

"Ben… my good friend… I should not like to see anything else happen to you. Rest well… and no more dreams!" He excused himself and followed after Josiah.

"They would not understand what we are about to discuss."

"You know where I am from, don't you."

"Yes, but where or when you come from matters not. What matters is that you are here… now. Your purpose will be revealed in time, but there are still things we must work on before you are ready. You have studied the Word of God your whole life… now it is time to *know* the Word… to *know* Me… and The Kingdom I bring. You must come to understand the sacrifice it takes to follow Me. Then… you will be ready to minister. Are you ready to give yourself completely to Me? It will take all of you to follow after Me, not just part of you." I thought I was ready."

"Yes Yeshua. I am ready."

"Will you give up being a Rabbi?"

"But… I thought that *was* my destiny. My heart has always had that desire."

"Two words, Benjamin… *I* and *my*. You must begin to understand, that if you follow Me, you are no longer your own. Only doing the Father's will is what matters... not *your* will, and not the desires of *your* own heart."

"I don't know... maybe I *can't* do it. Maybe I'm not ready."

"That's right, but through *Me*... you can be. What is the greatest commandment?"

"To love God with all your heart, soul, and strength."

"Yes... *ALL,* not some. Do you understand what I ask of you, and all others who choose to seek and serve God?" Through Me... this is possible. Now, you must get some rest. Tomorrow we go to Capernaum, then on to Jerusalem for the Passover."

"Thank you Yeshua. Thank you for saving my life."

"Goodnight Benjamin."

As Yeshua left the room, my thoughts turned inward to examine my soul. *He's right. There's still too much of ME left.* A great work had been done in my life, but there was so much more left to change. I will have to sacrifice everything. Immediately, a scripture came to mind. *To obey is better than sacrifice.* Isn't sacrifice obedience? *Ohhh... I'm so confused right now... just go to sleep Ben!*

Chapter 8: Repent and Be Baptized

The visit to Capernaum was a pleasant one. We met up with the disciples and some of their family members. It was amazing to see how real, and personal everyone was. I know in my own life... in reading the scriptures, I had always thought about how pure the disciples had to be. To be chosen by Yeshua, they had to be amazing. I found out they had an amazing love, and yet were all... far from being perfect! Yeshua however, was amazingly perfect! He was human, but also God. He laughed, He cried, He told jokes... clean ones of course. Oh, how I wanted to be like Him! I didn't want to leave Capernaum, but we had to move on

After the Sabbath, Simon and I headed for Jerusalem while Josiah, Gehazi and Menehem headed home. Our group of followers had grown. There were now close to thirty people following Yeshua. As we travelled south along the Jordan River, on the second day we came to a large broad section where it joined with another river to the west. Everyone stopped to rest. It was then, that Yeshua began to teach. He taught us about the love of God, and about forgiveness. He told us about The Kingdom and the riches of Heaven... and about treasures that were eternal. Yeshua made his way out into the river.

"The Kingdom of Heaven is near... repent and be baptized!" One by one, each person waded into the Jordan and stood before the Son of God to be baptized.

Do they realize who this is that baptizes them? I waded in and took my place in line. Slowly moving forward, I tried hard not to slip on the slimy rocks beneath my feet. This reminded me of Jacob's baptism, although it was quite different; a nice warm baptismal, perfect lighting and ambiance with soft music playing.

"Benjamin... what are you doing?" Sarah scolded me. "Put that away!" I closed the book I was reading and turned my attention to the boring dribble that was being played out before us. Each person was giving their *testimony,* some of which were a little too long... if you asked me.

"I was going to stop when Jacob got up there." I whispered.

"It's not polite to the others... you should try and listen to what they are saying. You might learn something!" I doubted if I would learn anything, although I suppose it was a *little* rude to be reading while these people were being dunked. Next up was Jacob.

"Jacob Messler? Come on in son." Jacob eased down the steps of the baptismal and made his way to the microphone.

"Hi, my name is Jake. I know I am only nine years old, but I want to tell you what Jesus has done for me. I suppose I'm not old enough to have committed any of the really *bad* sins that are out there..." The congregation laughed. He continued. "... but I know now that I have been selfish, deceitful, and disobedient. I used to not listen to my parents very well and always wanted everything done *my* way." Sarah grabbed my hand and squeezed. "Since I let Jesus take control of my life, I no longer want it *my* way... I want it *His* way! I got saved last month at Bible Camp and I will never be the same again!"

Sarah began to cry as the youth pastor baptized our son. I, on the other hand, was touched by Jacob's words… but was oblivious to the meaning behind them.

I faced Yeshua, wishing Jake was here to see this. As I looked in his eyes, I saw such love and compassion. I was overwhelmed with shame from every instance of selfish desire and pride I'd ever had. I was overcome with the knowledge of just how insignificant I was. My intellect… my self-righteousness, and my accomplishments in life were nothing. Nothing!

My whole life was all about Benjamin Messler. I felt so dirty! I lowered my head and looked at the swirling water around me. I was so unworthy to even look in his eyes. Yeshua put his hand under my chin and lifted my head so I could look in his eyes again. Tears began to flow. Yeshua looked around at the small gathering.

"This man stands before me with genuine sorrow in his heart. True repentance will produce fruit, and every tree that does not produce fruit will be cut down and cast in the fire. Repent and be baptized!"

I went down in the water, feeling the sins of my past being washed away with the current. No longer was I a man of the World, I was a man of God… a Follower of The Messiah. Yeshua embraced me.

"I love you Ben."

I was too choked up to speak. I nodded a response, and he knew how I felt. I joined the others and was met with warm embraces and praises to God. I was elated! It was as if my eyes were opened for the first time. There was now no doubt in my mind. Yeshua *IS* the Son of God!

While drying out in the sun, I heard a commotion. I sat up and looked over to where it was coming from. There were some heated words exchanged, and some people leaving and heading south along the Jordan. I couldn't see Yeshua, but Simon and Nathaniel were close by discussing something. I rose to my feet and quickly joined them and their conversation.

"What's going on?" Nathaniel was the first to respond to me.

"Yeshua has instructed us to follow a route through Samaria instead of following the Jordan south to Jerusalem. We are to stay in the city of Sychar and wait for him there." Simon was very uneasy about the whole thing.

"Why? Why must we endanger our lives by staying there? It is a melting pot of sin and guile! I am not going!" Simon seemed quite serious about his decision. I had to reassure him.

"Simon, you and I have come so far... please don't give up! Yeshua would not send us there unless there was a reason for it. We must trust him." He just shook his head and looked at the ground.

"Ben, have you ever been to Sychar? Do you know what type of city it is? What type of people live there?" I was unfazed by his remarks. I turned to Nathaniel.

"Nathaniel... do you trust Yeshua?"

"Yes, I do. I will follow him anywhere!"

"I feel the same... Simon, you *must* trust him... please, come with us!" Simon rubbed his chin, contemplating his decision.

"You are an odd man Benjamin! In spite of my feelings, who am I to place my own understanding on this? I look at you can't help but be inspired to do so. Yes! We will go to Sychar!"

Chapter 9: Samaritan Grace

We finally made it to the main road headed south to Sychar. Only about twenty people were left from the original crowd from Capernaum. Those who headed south along the east side of the Jordan were disappointed that Yeshua would choose the road through Samaria. Obviously, their trust in him was too weak to forbear. Our group was obediently driving on, but some still grumbled about it.

The road made it easier going, and once reaching Sychar, we were to stop and spend the night there. Although the Sabbath was that evening, there would be no Synagogue to worship in come the morning.

Tensions rose as we approached the small city. Traffic on the road was increasing with tradesman and travelers. Many just quietly stared at our group as they passed by, while others would travel off road, giving us a wide birth. To ease his apprehension, Simon took up conversation with me.

"When do you think the next miracle will happen?" I smiled at him.

"Well… you're looking at one! My life has been changed miraculously!"

"Oh, I know. I just want to see another miracle like the water changing into wine. I'm sure, in Jerusalem, we will see something happen!"

"It may be sooner than that. We will be staying in Sychar tonight! That alone will be a miracle if we live through it!" I laughed at my comment, but Simon found no humor in it whatsoever.

It was hopeless. Simon was drawn to the extravagant miracles and dreaded the thought of being around Samaritans. I can understand where he is coming from. However, to me... the miracle that happens within, is far greater than anything to behold externally. I just want to know God with all that is within me. I want to know my destiny... whatever that may be.

Sychar... for its size, was very busy. Apparently, it was a popular stop on a major trade route. The main square was a sizable melting pot of commerce. There were the typical sales of fruit, oil, clothing, meat, and souvenirs. Also available were the gamblers who dealt in dice games and pigeon races. Then there were the moneychangers, prostitutes, and drunkards... your typical Las Vegas of the times. As we pushed through the crowds, Nathaniel commented on the variety of people.

"Hang on to your purse brother, there are those who would take it and you not know the difference! After the Sabbath, we will buy as much food as we can carry. Jerusalem is very expensive... especially during the Passover!"

"Where will we stay tonight?" Simon asked. "It looks as if lodging may be difficult to find... and *safe* lodging, even more so!"

"If we are not satisfied with anything here, we will have to find shelter outside the city."

Nathaniel had a way of taking charge. He was quick on his feet, and this group trusted him in the absence of Yeshua.

I was lost in thought and trying to process everything Nathaniel was saying, when two men bumped into me, almost knocking me over. Both men reeked of alcohol and bad spirit.

"What are you doing fool!" This brutish man spoke in an Egyptian dialect. His colleague continued.

"Watch where you are going!"

He shoved me with all his might... sending me flying into the crowd and knocking over some innocent bystanders. Now I'm not one to back down from a fight, but something inside of me had compassion for these two individuals. First of all, I outweighed them both by at least fifty pounds. Secondly, they were obviously drunk. So drunk, that they had difficulty standing. I attempted a peaceful alternative.

"I'm not looking for any trouble..." They showed surprise in my linguistic abilities. I knew most Egyptian dialects as well. "The crowd is pressing in all around us. If I accidentally bumped into you, I am sorry. I beg your forgiveness."

The larger of the two stepped forward... nose to nose with me. His breath stunk of stale beer and rotten teeth. His adornment of earrings, jewelry, and tattoos did nothing for his appearance but intensify his grotesque demeanor.

"You may beg Pig! Kneel before me and beg!"

He turned to his friend and laughed. When he returned his gaze, a look of surprise filled his face. He was expecting me to cower before him, but I was holding my ground with a simple stare.

"You mock me?"

He pulled back his arm and made an attempt at a haymaker. I easily saw it coming, so I ducked. He followed through with his punch and landed in a heap on the ground. Those who stood around watching burst into laughter.

The other man boiled with anger as he ran towards me in a rage, screaming. I stepped aside and watched him dive head long into the dirt and skid to a halt at the feet of the mob around us. With that move, the laughter became almost deafening!

The two men sat on the ground, too embarrassed to continue. I reached down and offered them a hand up. The grotesque man with all the jewelry, accepted. The smaller man scurried away like a mouse and got lost in the horde of people.

"Why did you offer me your hand? I wanted to kill you... yet you show me goodwill?" What compassion I had for this man before, was now multiplied.

"Because when I was undeserving of mercy and compassion... I was given it. What is your name?"

"Psusennes." [2] When faced with friendship, this man melted into one of innocence and bewilderment, rather than anger and malice.

"Come Psusennes... will you join us?" Nathaniel and Simon gaffed in disbelief. Their eyes said... *Are you crazy?*

"Me? You want me to join you? Why?"

"Do you want to be free? I know a man who can give you freedom from all your pain and emptiness."

I didn't know where the words were coming from, but they were hitting their mark. Psusennes started welling up with tears. Just then, Simon yanked my arm and pulled me away.

"What are you doing? He is not a Jew! He is Egyptian scum! What do you mean inviting this vulgar man to join us? Nathaniel imposed his own plight.

"He cannot join us! Most of our traveling companions will not allow it!" The others stood behind him in profuse agreement.

---

[2] Pronounced su-se-nees

"Then I will find a different place to stay this evening. I will meet you here in the square after the Sabbath to continue on to Jerusalem, if you will have us."

They could not believe what they were hearing, and I could not believe what I was saying. I was really stepping out on a limb here... and didn't know why. It just felt right to do it. Religious bigotry ran strong in these times. No amount of reading in the modern world could have prepared me for experiencing this firsthand.

"Are you sure Benjamin? This man is a trader from Egypt. They are crafty *and* dangerous. Please reconsider."

"Simon, you must understand... Yeshua came to give life to everyone, not just the Jews."

"Well let Yeshua deal with... that guile man. Besides, the Sabbath is upon us. You wish to spend it with that heathen? They are full of sorcery and deception!"

"Simon. Look at him. Do you not now see a broken man, seeking... wanting more from life? Yeshua can give him that! Don't you see?"

"No... I don't see! Be careful my friend. If you are not in the square after the Sabbath is over; I will begin to search the ditches for your body!"

He forced a grin, but I could still see the worry in his eyes. Simon ended our conversation.

"Yasher Koach."[3]

"Shalom"[4]

Psusennes seemed quite sober now. He said he had lodging, so I followed him through the square and down a maze of narrow

---

[3] Meaning straight strength or may you have strength

[4] Meaning peace, hello or goodbye

side streets. I hoped I could find my way back. If I was in need of escaping my situation, it would be nice to know.

"Are you sure you have room for me?"

"I will give up my own bed for you, if need be. You have shown me such undeserved kindness."

We made one last turn and came to an inn. The noise coming from inside was boisterous. Psusennes shot out a warning. "Just as your friends were not accepting of me, you may find some in here that feel the same way toward you. Stay close… I won't let anything happen to you."

He opened the door and we entered the dimly lit inn and tavern. I was hit with a wave of hot air mingled with the smell of things I cared not to know about. I was feeling all eyes on me as we made our way through the sea of drunken traders and tawdry characters. I was yearning for the feel of my 9mm Berretta strapped to my waist. Psusennes found who he was looking for. He appeared to be the inn keeper. Psusennes spoke with him briefly. I couldn't hear them over the clamorous partiers, but his friends' interest was piqued. He looked at me then grabbed my arm and led me to the back of the inn to a separate area. I was beginning to wonder if I should be afraid or not when I saw the most unusual site. In the back room, there were a small group of men, and a few women of ill-repute crowded around a man speaking to them. I was shocked! Here was Yeshua among the worst of the worst in Sychar! The room reeked of alcohol and body odor… and if I weren't mistaken, the smell of urine. I was having a hard time holding down my lunch of figs and berries. While Yeshua, on the other hand, sat right in the middle of them all… pouring out the Fathers heart. What a man of compassion!

"Do you know this man? Is He the one you were telling Psusennes about?" The inn keeper's voice wavered with agitation. "You must speak with Him… tell Him to leave! I am losing business… I need paying customers!" He walked back to the front in a huff.

"Pay him no mind, he is always this way. Worried about losing customers, yet he is never lacking of business. Is this Yeshua?"

"Yes… yes, this is Yeshua."

"My colleague says He has been here all-day sharing words for all who will listen. He speaks of things that are amazing and tells what is in a man's mind and heart! Is this true? Can He do these things?"

I was still wondering how He got here so quickly. We only arrived here a while ago… and He has been here *all* day?

"Yes… He can do those things… and a lot more apparently!"

I looked at Yeshua in a newer light, and I thanked God for the opportunity to have been here right now. The look on each one of their faces was a sight to see. There was a glow of wonderment and awe about them. The same look a baby gives his mother when she sings to him or woos him. Yeshua came for the sick and the broken… for those who were in need of a physician.

"Will you sit with me and listen to Him?" Psusennes nodded in agreement. We sat on the floor, up against the wall, and melted into the host of curious onlookers.

"May I sit here with you?" I looked up to see Simon standing there. "I followed you… thought you needed some looking after." He smiled. It seems I could, after all, count on him when I least expected it.

"Simon! So good to see you! Do you see who we have found?" It was only then that he realized who it was holding the attention of everyone in the room.

"How did… how?"

"I know… how did Yeshua end up *here*? There's more. He has been here since this morning!" Simon's mouth dropped open in disbelief.

"But… He couldn't! No one could journey that far, that fast!"

"You wanted another miracle? There it is. Now… do you see why He wanted us to come through Samaria? Look around the room, what do you see?" Simon slid his back down the wall and sat down beside me. "Do you see the miracle of transformation taking place in these people here?" Simon was quick to answer.

"No, I see drunkards, pickpockets, harlots and lowly traders." Simon looked at Psusennes as he said that.

Psusennes burned his eyes into Simon. After a moment of looking around a second time, Simon's countenance began to change. His eyes began to soften a little.

"No… I see hurting, lost people. I see hope in their eyes."

"I am beginning to see a little hope in you as well, Simon. Listen to what Yeshua is saying."

We turned our attention to the Son of God who humbled himself enough to come and teach in this putrid, disgusting place… to show love and compassion to those who would not otherwise find it.

"Listen to Me… Do not judge, so you will not be judged. Do not condemn others, and you will not be condemned. Be forgiving, and you will find yourself forgiven. Be generous, and you will be given much. A good measure, pressed down, shaken together and running over. You see, what you have been giving, will be given to you."

What Yeshua was saying was hitting home with Simon. I was amazed at the timing involved in this teaching. A few moments ago, Simon was judging these people. Now, he was being judged.

"Can a blind man lead another? Will they not both stumble or fall into a pit? Someone who is taught... is not above his teacher. Why do you look at the fault of others and not see your own? You see a speck of sawdust in your brother's eye, yet you have a log in your own eye! Do you see? You must first remove what is in your own eye before you can help your brother with what is in his. Do not be a hypocrite!"

Those gathered around Yeshua were in awe of his words. Some were crying, while others were simply quiet.

"Consider this. A wise man built his house upon a rock. He dug deep for his foundation. When the rains came and the wind beat against the house, it was not shaken. A foolish man built his house upon sand. When the rains came and the wind beat against his house, it collapsed. It was completely destroyed! If you hear my words, and obey them, you will survive the storms of life, for you have a firm foundation in Me. If you do not hear and obey my words, you will be as the man who built his house upon the sand."

The meeting was suddenly interrupted by a rather large man, yelling as he pushed others aside.

"What goes on here? My brother says no one is buying drink! We are losing profit and *YOU*... Rabbi, seem to be the cause of it!"

He made his way through the host and stood before Yeshua. A woman, who apparently was familiar with the man, stepped near him and spoke up.

"Please! Don't harm him! Listen to what he speaks of..."

The man growled in anger and drew back his arm to backhand her.

"Quiet woman!"

He swung to strike, but his hand was caught mid stride with a loud clap... as a firm hand grasped his wrist.

"No need to hit the woman. She has done nothing."

Yeshua spoke in almost a whisper but had the effect of a bullhorn. Everyone heard it and waited for a response from the furious man. The sweat began to bead up on the man's forehead, and his body began to quake as he struggled with all his might against the power holding him. Yeshua looked at him with those piercing eyes… those eyes of unmistakable love and mercy. He loosened his grip. The man fell to his knees and began sobbing. Having been faced with the shame in his life, he repented and worshiped Yeshua.

"I tell you… I am the bread of life. All who come to Me will never go hungry, and all who believe in Me will never thirst. This man has known hunger. This man has known thirst. Do you see that I am the bread that satisfies, and the water that quenches every thirst? I am the light of the world. Whoever follows after Me will never walk in darkness but will have the light of life."

All were amazed at his words, and in awe of what had just transpired. As the hours passed, more and more people showed up to hear the Galilean speak. Many were saved, to include the inn keeper, his brother, and my new friend Psusennes!

There may not have been a Synagogue in the city of Sychar, but the inn was filled the morning of the Sabbath. New believers in The Messiah were gathered together to worship God and hear from Yeshua. Though many were tired from such a late night, the energy filled the air with electricity.

There was standing room only. Apparently, news had spread in the wee hours of the morning. There were many more people present that morning than were here the night before. Hope radiated from every face. They longed for Yeshua… They longed for the Truth.

"Benjamin." I turned and faced Yeshua. He embraced me and smiled. "You have listened to God's voice. Obedience bears much fruit! Because of your obedience, Psusennes, as well as others, have come to know the truth!" I had never felt quite as fulfilled in my life as I did in that moment. What a wonderful thing to be a small part of.

"Yeshua, it is very crowded this morning. How will everyone hear your words? The inn is full and there are so many more that are waiting outside in the street!"

"I have spoken with the inn keeper. I will go up on the roof and speak to everyone from up there. I will need your help. Will you and Simon guide the others to the outside?"

"Yes... of course. I will find Simon and do that now."

Yeshua made his way up the stairs. After locating Simon, we proceeded to direct the crowds of people outside where Yeshua began to teach. Some came out of curiosity, then left. Others stayed, and many were saved.

The day was filled with The Word, miracles, deliverance... what a morning! This, at the grass roots level, *is* The Kingdom. Not the brick and mortar. Not the programs and special classes. Not the *Christian Cruises* and concert venues. *This*... this is what The Messiah intended... to be the representation of The Kingdom of God. It's interaction with people, its commitment, and loving devotion to The Messiah on a daily basis.

My eyes were being opened to a whole new dimension. Within myself, there rose up a deep fear.

How can I live up to this? How can I give everything, just as The Messiah does? How can I shove my own selfish desires aside and live like Him?

The sun was cresting the horizon as Simon, Yeshua and I made our way into the marketplace to meet the others. Traders were quietly setting up shop as the crickets gave up their song and retired for the day. Meat was hung up, fruit was stacked neatly, and traders put on their game face to prepare for work.

I couldn't help but wonder if Nathaniel and the rest of the followers would even show this morning. In the far corner of the plaza was a huddle of shadows that looked familiar. They had made it after all! As we approached, Nathaniel's face showed great surprise and relief; seeing Yeshua walking with us was a boost of morale to him and the others. Spirits were lifted and smiles were gleaming as greetings were exchanged. Nathaniel grasped Simon and I, one in each arm.

"You are alive! There was much speculation as to whether or not you would be here this morning!" Simon was the first to speak.

"We have many testimonies to share with you! We are more than alive! You would not believe the miracles we have seen these past days!"

"Come then.... share with us as we walk." Nathaniel... always eager for a testimony soaked everything up like a sponge. As Simon unfolded the events, a look of sorrow came over Nathaniel. "Forgive me for doubting." He looked at Yeshua. "I have thought Samaritans to be a lesser people, unworthy of God and all that is His. ***I*** am the lesser for not believing in the depth of your love. Yeshua... I will not doubt again!" Yeshua embraced him.

Chapter 10: First Jerusalem Passover

Jerusalem! Oh holy city! My eyes were moist as I beheld the holy city of our God! The roads were thick with travelers, and the dust just as thick on my feet. Tired, weary, and smelling like a teenage kid just out of gym class, we made our way up to Jerusalem.

I have seen this city many times, but now... it holds new meaning for me. Gone is the bitterness toward my father and my heritage. Present is the love and purpose that The Messiah has instilled in me. Yeshua was now walking beside me.

"Beautiful.... isn't it?" Yeshua said. I nodded in agreement. "If you think it's beautiful now, wait until The Kingdom of God is made manifest! It will be perfect...."

His voice trailed off and I caught a sense of grief in it. To think that Yeshua's life on earth would end here.... rejected by his own people. Suddenly I realized, for the first time in my life, the sacrifice He was about to give for all mankind.

"Yeshua... how can You go on.... knowing what's ahead?" He turned to me. His eyes were wet with tears as a smile came to His face.

"Because of my love for *you* Ben. My suffering will all be worth it to know that you and others will be restored to what the Father intended for His children."

It's one thing to hear about Yeshua's love from reading the New Testament; it's another to hear Him say to your face that He loves you, and that His suffering is *for* you! The reality of what He will go through at his crucifixion was very sobering to me. Living here... in this time with Yeshua, put's a whole new light on what He will do for all of us. I prayed that I would be gone by the time this happens.

It was hard to believe so many people could fit within the walls of the city. It was like Black Friday without the stampedes. Crowds mulled along in a somewhat orderly fashion... not in a hurry or frenzied state; which was good, considering the size of our group. John squeezed up alongside me and offered some conversation.

"Did you expect this? Have you ever been to Jerusalem for the Passover?"

"No... I haven't," I said.

"It will be an exciting few days!" Simon, who was on the other side of me moved close so I could hear him over the crowd.

"Benjamin. We will be to the temple soon. It is a sight to behold!"

I smiled and nodded in agreement. Having seen the Western Wall before in my time, I was truly anxious to see it now in its complete state.

We rounded a corner and began our assent to the temple. Yeshua was now quite a ways ahead of me with some of the others. Slowly, we went up the steps and entered the temple courts. It was filled to capacity with men selling cattle, sheep and doves. Money changers sat at tables providing their services... not without a price, of course.

In a corner to my left, I spotted Yeshua making something out of some scrap pieces of cord. *The whip!* I thought. *Of course! The temple courts! The money changers! This is about to get interesting.*

Yeshua had a look on His face I had not yet seen. Anger! His eyes burned like fire. As He made his way across the court, Peter walked along side asking Him

"Master! What are You going to do?"

Peter stopped short as Yeshua approached the money changing tables. The men were counting their profits and laughing amongst themselves. One man took notice as eye contact was made with the Son of God. Suddenly, his attention was drawn to the whip in Yeshua's hand. His eyes shown wide with fear.... The realization of what was about to happen, came too slowly to react. Yeshua came down hard with the whip and struck the man on the back as he turned to run. The man sitting next to him fell backwards to the ground and covered his face as Yeshua proceeded to turn the whip on him.

Yeshua turned over more tables. Money went flying everywhere as people scrambled to scoop up what they could run with.

Yeshua shouted, "Get this out of here! How can you turn My Father's house into a place to buy and sell?"

Next He turned on the sellers of livestock.... knocking over the makeshift fencing and setting the sheep and cattle free. Men tried to stop him but were met with a zeal they could not contend against. Within two minutes the court was emptied.

Yeshua stood in the center, breathing hard as He let the whip fall to the ground. The disciples and other followers stood around with their mouths hanging open, not sure what to think of the situation. A group of about five men approached as soon as the whip hit ground. One man exclaimed.

"Can you give us a sign or a miracle that will prove your authority for doing all this? Has God himself given you the right to ruin the commerce of these men?"

Yeshua raised His head, and with a quiet voice said,

"Destroy this temple... and I will raise it again in three days"

"What? Three days?" The leader of the group of men said. "It has taken forty-six years to build this temple, and you think you could raise it in three days?" He turned to the others and laughed, "He thinks he can rebuild it in three days!" The men who had gathered around began to scorn and mock Yeshua as they walked away. John and Peter walked up to Yeshua.

"Master," said John. "What shall we do?"

"I know what to do," said Peter. "Give me that whip and I'll flail those pompous Jews to a pile of mush! I'll finish the work that Yeshua started!" Peter bent down to get the whip. Yeshua gently placed a hand on his arm.

"Peter," Yeshua softly scolded him. "There is no need for you to finish anything. If they want to see miraculous signs, they only need to open their eyes. Come. Let us worship together in the temple."

Many people that day saw miraculous signs. Some believed... while others did not. Yeshua was right. If they see it with their own eyes, yet reject the Truth, they will not believe. It's a matter of the heart.... not something seen in the flesh.

That night, we talked amongst ourselves as we ate a few small morsels. The room we were staying in was dimly lit... by one small oil lamp. Great shadows fell on the wall and waved ever so slightly with the movement of flame. The doorway was covered with a dark cloth that looked like a portal into a dark world of night. I was fixed on the door. Staring at it... wondering if it would swallow me up, when all of a sudden, a hand appeared and moved the curtain aside. A man of distinction, clothed in the robe of a Pharisee, stepped through the doorway. Those who were close to slumber were stirring as the man surveyed the room. His gaze fell on Yeshua, and he approached him.

"Greetings Rabbi." He spoke quietly, as if he thought someone outside may be listening. "My name is Nicodemus. I am a member of the Jewish Council. You have been stirring up quite a following in this holy city today!" Yeshua acknowledged him with a smile.

"We know that you are a teacher who has come from God. It is evident from the miracles performed by you today. God is truly with you. I should like to know more about your teachings and the kingdom of which you talk about." Yeshua motioned for him to sit beside him.

"Nicodemus, I want you to understand something. No one can see The Kingdom of God unless he is born again."

Nicodemus probed Yeshua with his eyes then said, "How can a man be born again when he is old? No man can enter into his mother's womb for a second time to be born!"

"I tell you the truth; no one can enter The Kingdom of God unless he is born of water *AND* the Spirit. Flesh gives birth to flesh, but Spirit gives birth to spirit."

Yeshua shook his head at the Pharisees' reaction.

"You should not be surprised at my saying, 'you must be born again.' The wind blows wherever it wants to. You hear the sound, but you cannot tell where it comes from or where it is going. So it is with everyone born of the Spirit."

"How can this be?" Nicodemus asked again with a sigh of frustration.

"You are Israel's teacher, and you do not understand these things? Nicodemus... we speak of what we know, and we testify to what we have seen, but *STILL* you people do not accept our testimony!

I have spoken to you about earthly things and you do not believe; how then will you believe if I speak of heavenly things? No one has ever gone to heaven except the One who came from heaven; the Son of Man. Just as Moses lifted up the snake in the desert, so the Son of Man must be lifted up, that everyone who believes in Him may have eternal life."

It seemed as though he were talking to a brick wall. The harder that Nicodemus reasoned with his intellect, the less his spirit could interpret the heart of the matter at hand. I felt sorry for him. I believed he was truly seeking, but he let his mind get in the way of his heart. Yeshua continued.

"God so loves this world that He Has given his only Son, that whosoever believes in Him should not perish but have eternal life. Don't you see? God did not send His Son into the world to condemn the world, but to save it... through Him. If mankind would believe in Him, they would not be condemned, but if they do not believe in Him, they stand condemned already. You must believe in the name of God's One and only Son. Let me try and explain it another way . . . Light has come into the world, but men love the darkness because their deeds are evil. Everyone who does evil hates the light and will not come *into* the light because their evil deeds will be exposed. Nicodemus, if you live by the truth and come into the light . . . You will plainly see that what I have done has been done through God."

Long into the night this went on. Nicodemus left Yeshua with an invitation to his home so that he may teach some others on the Council. The disciples were not too keen on the idea, but they were beginning to understand that the message of Yeshua was not just for them. I slept soundly that night. The more I got to know the heart of Yeshua, the more at peace I was in my own soul. I couldn't help but think how much Nicodemus and me were alike. My intellect got in the way for many years. It was all about knowledge, and study, and pride. Thank God for His mercy. What a gift to be able to come back in time and experience all this for myself. On the following Sabbath, Yeshua and a few of us went to the house of Nicodemus. It was a very nice house. The kind of house that screamed... *don't touch anything*! We met in a small courtyard where there were at least ten more Pharisees as well as some who were not part of the Council.

It was very evident that some came to try and discount what Yeshua stood for, while some seemed honestly intrigued by him. They really wanted the truth. As we sat around the room, a man approached Yeshua and knelt before him. He was suffering from dropsy. His limbs were horribly swollen. It looked painful.

"Is it lawful to heal on the Sabbath?"

Yeshua obviously was setting them up. They stayed quiet and would not respond. Yeshua took hold of the man's hand and healed him in their presence. His arms and legs seemed to deflate like a balloon. The skin was now smooth and new looking and the swelling non-existent.

"Go.... You are made well."

There was a low rumble of voices as the religious men conferred with one another then went deathly silent. Yeshua broke the silence.

"If one of you has a son or an ox that falls into a well on the Sabbath day, will you not pull him out right away?"

They remained quiet. It was obvious that they could not discount what had just happened. Yeshua surveyed the room and began to notice the places of prominence.

"When someone invites you to a wedding feast... do not take the place of honor, it may not have been reserved for you. Then you will be humiliated if someone more important than you arrives and you are made to move to a lower place of prominence. Instead, take the lowest place so that in your humbleness you may be exalted when the master comes to you and says 'Please.... sit here as my honored guest'. I see that it is common among you to try and place yourselves in a privileged position. As you arrived, it was evident that most of you considered yourselves *first* among the others and fought to be nearest to the host."

I looked around the room and saw the offense written in the blushing faces of those near Nicodemus. Yeshua had struck a nerve, and half of the men immediately got up and left in a huff. Yeshua turned to Nicodemus and continued.

"When you invite people into your home for dinner or a luncheon, do not always invite your friends. Do not invite your relatives or your rich neighbors; if you do...yes, you will be repaid. But instead, invite the poor and needy.... the crippled, lame and blind. They cannot repay you, and that is good, for your reward will come at the resurrection of the righteous." Nicodemus was sincerely moved.

"Yeshua.... You have taught me much these last few days and I have been rebuked many times by your words. I will truly seek to do what is right."

Nicodemus left us with an invitation to return at any time and promised to put into action what Yeshua had spoken about. As we departed Jerusalem, I marveled at all the miracles that took place while we were there. Seeing those things can sure build your faith. I wished I could stay in this time. My life was fulfilled here. I had no desire to go back.

Chapter 11: Colony of Lepers

Many more followers had joined our band of believers. It was getting more difficult to be organized. Nathaniel tried his best to keep some sense of order but finally resorted to just concentrating on our original group and let the others fend for themselves. It seemed as though other leaders were rising to the occasion, so he put the responsibilities in their hands.

I could see Nathaniel in the modern world. He would be a top-ranking CEO of a large company . . . Fortune 500 all the way! I wouldn't wish that upon *him* though. Corruption of the 21st century would taint even him, I'm sure.

Not far out of Jerusalem, one of the men traveling beside me noticed something strange.

"Did you see that?" The man pointed to the trees alongside the road. I looked and saw nothing.

"There!"

He pointed again. This time I saw it. There was a man in a dark tunic wearing a veil that covered his head. He moved silently through the trees gliding quickly from one to the next and stopping to hide behind each one. The sun was beginning to set and it cast and eerie look on the whole scene.

Suddenly, the strange form burst into the open.... running at Yeshua. The disciples walking with Yeshua were stunned and froze in their tracks. Falling down at the feet of Yeshua, the man screamed

Yeshua... Yeshua... have mercy on me!"

His hands reach toward Yeshua as he lay prone on the ground. It was then that I noticed his hands. They were loosely wrapped with dirty rags, but enough showed to reveal his Leprosy. Everyone stepped back to put distance between themselves and this man. Yeshua responded by kneeling down and grabbing the man's hand. He pulled him to his feet and gazed past the veil covering the man's face.

"Why do you ask for mercy and not healing?" Everyone held his breathe as they awaited a response from this poor man.

"My leprosy is a curse that I can live with... for I am deserving of such. But my soul bears a grief that I cannot bear. I cannot live with the sin of my past. I have done a horrible thing for which I am truly sorry... Please... take this weight from me, for I can bear it no longer!"

"Your faith is great. Mercy and forgiveness, I have for you... Be made whole!"

Yeshua reached up and tore the veil from the man's head. The man who stood before us all was no longer plagued with a filthy soul *or* body. The leprous man was clean! Smooth new skin replaced the old. The tears glistened on his cheeks, and his eyes were bright and joyful as he touched his face and realized that *two* gifts were given to him that day.

"Please! You must come with me. Up here, through this canyon, is the Leper Colony that I came from. More people are in great need of You! Many have not been able to hold their families for years. They can only gaze from a distance as their loved ones bring food for them to eat. I myself have a son that I have yet to hold in my own arms. He is now walking! Now I may run with him, and hold him, and kiss him!"

The new man in The Messiah embraced Yeshua and sobbed.

"Please... will you come?" Yeshua smiled and agreed.

Some of us went with Yeshua while others made camp and stayed behind. Jonathan, for that was the leper's name, told his story as we journeyed through the twisting canyon.

After marrying his wife, she conceived a child. She was still pregnant when Jonathan was discovered to have Leprosy. He was then isolated and brought to the Colony. He had only seen his son grow from a distance as she often, brought food to him.

It was only a few hours ago that some people at the gate had told him of a man known as Yeshua, and that this healer was traveling this way. Jonathan was the only one brave enough to venture outside the compound and seek out Yeshua.

He ran as fast as he could only to end up at the edge of the trees with a paralyzing fear overtaking him. He watched and hid, not only seeing his wife and son's face flash before his eyes, but also the face of the man whose life he took a few years earlier. This man had tried to take his food. He went at Jonathan with a knife. A struggle ensued, and Jonathan was forever stained with the blood of that man on his hands.

We saw torches lit just ahead and began to smell the stench of an overpopulated colony of lepers. We arrived at the gate and received a stern warning.

"Come no further! We are unclean!" the man said.

Jonathan approached the gate causing the man to retreat to the shadows.

"Simeon.... It's me, Jonathan!"

He stretched his arm through the gate, showing the ring that he used to wear around his neck, as proof to the bewildered leper. Simeon crept forward; his face still shadowed in the darkness.

"Can this be? Is it really you my friend?"

"Yes Simeon! Yeshua has healed me and I have brought him so that you may be made well too! Open the gate and you will be set free my friend!"

The latch was lifted and so was the burden on so many lost souls that night. All came to know the power of healing. Not just in the physical, but spirits set free from the clutches of hell.

Torches snuffed out.... and little sleep ensued. The rays of dawn woke the few left sleeping in the colony. Many, after healing and teaching, set off in the dark for home. They wanted to see their families again. After years of being held captive by their disease, their first concern fell on seeing their loved ones again. Some chose to stay and follow Yeshua. Our new friend Jonathan was one who left.... can't say that I blame him. Although, I wished he would have decided to stay. He was truly a unique man and it would have been great to get to know him better.

As we gathered together for our journey back to the main road, I was astonished at how this crowd of people keeps growing. Simon was amazed as well.

"Benjamin. Do you think this will keep happening like this? The followers keep growing and growing! How can this be managed?" I stepped up to the question without any hesitation.

"God only knows.... and only He could orchestrate such a marvelous thing. We must trust in our Father to provide in all things and keep learning from Yeshua. I too am overwhelmed, but God is greater than all my unbelief."

As we came in to view of Nathaniel and the rest of those who stayed behind, I was surprised to see Jonathan and his wife and child standing there with the biggest smiles on their faces. They just glowed! Along with him were many more of the lepers who were healed, and *their* families. Yeshua called the disciples over to him so that he could give instructions. He stood there a moment just looking at them and smiling. He looked to the heavens and exclaimed,

"Father... thank you for such a bountiful harvest! Guide us onward and show us your kingdom!" He then looked each of the disciples in the eyes and spoke.

"Do you see? People are thirsting for the Truth.... They are in desperate need of only what my Father can give them. You must now stand in your calling as my disciples. They must be baptized. You will baptize those who wish to follow the will of the Father. Teach them what I have taught you about The Kingdom and love them as I have loved you." Peter was the first to express their collective doubts to Yeshua.

"Yeshua.... We are not Rabbi's or great men of God. We are just fisherman." His voice quivered with the thought of the responsibility. "How can we do this?"

"Peter, you must trust me. You have seen me... just do what I've done. Rely on the Father to reveal the Truth. You are fishers of men now. Reap the harvest that is before you. These people need direction and you can show them the way to go. All of you..." He now spoke to all of the disciples.

"All of you have seen Me, so you have seen the Father. Show them the Father. Baptize them and disciple them, then we must return to Sychar. Through Me you will all do great and mighty things.... Just believe." Yeshua embraced them then went off to pray.

Jonathan and his family approached. His wife was glowing, and his son was held in his arms tightly as they greeted us.

"Benjamin.... Simon, this is my wife Dara and my son Jona." The boy's eyes were wide with excitement.

"Are you Yeshua?" Jonathan laughed and corrected his son.

"No, Jona. Neither of these men are Yeshua. I showed you Yeshua earlier, remember? This is Benjamin..." He pointed to me "... and this is Simon. They are two friends whom I became very close to last night. They travel with Yeshua."

"We are going with Yeshua too... right Father?" Jonathan turned his attention to us again.

"We have decided to follow Yeshua."

"Yes!" His wife exclaimed. "We owe our lives to him! This Yeshua has made all things new again!" Tears were streaming down her face as she spoke. "He gave us our lives back!" She was exuberant! Jonathan continued.

"You must tell us more.... more of what Yeshua was telling me last night. I want Dara to hear it." Just then, Nathaniel called us all over.

"Come! All who wish to be baptized! Up ahead is water... only a short way!"

We all began to move in the direction led by the disciples. There was an excitement weighing heavy on the crowd. Around the bend in the road was a pool of water that was fed by a small stream. It was like an oasis. The beautiful trees held plenty of shade for most of the group, and the cool clear water was inviting to sore and tired feet.

Peter and John waded out into the water and began to share from their hearts the message of Yeshua The Messiah. They gave testimony as to the life changes that were made. They gave witness to the miracles they had seen. They gave words of enrichment and fulfillment. They gave love. People began to weep as each one waded into the waters of that pool just North of Jerusalem.

There were those who stood back and watched from behind the crowd of people... their faces shown a look of disdain, not one of concurrence. I walked over to the group and questioned them directly.

"Welcome.... Why are you here? Are you willing to be baptized?" No one spoke, they only stared at me. I asked again. "Why are you here?" One man finally answered me.

"We are concerned that many of these who follow this Yeshua, are being baptized by him instead of John. We came to see for ourselves."

"You have not come for yourselves. Who sent you?" It was obvious that these men were here to cause division, not to simply observe. Andrew, Peter's brother stepped up behind me.

"Benjamin, are these men here to be baptized?" The look on his face showed that he was aware of the spirit behind these men and came to back me up.

"No Andrew... in fact I think they are leaving now."

The men took the hint and walked off whispering amongst themselves. I turned to Andrew.

"I believe they were here to cause division. They said that John should be baptizing instead of Yeshua."

"Well they would be surprised to learn that Yeshua isn't even doing the baptizing... Peter and John are. Many more have stopped on their passage to see what is happening, and *they* are now waiting to be delivered from sin and be baptized as well. More of us are needed to help. Come."

The crowd seemed to never end. By mid-day, all of us were exhausted. Between the baptizing, ministry, and teaching, there was no time to breathe. Just as soon as we all settled down to rest and eat something, Yeshua came back from his time of prayer.

"We must now leave for Sychar."

There was an audible groan from the group of followers close to Yeshua. Some stood and began to march obediently toward Samaria. However, division was not far from those who were still consumed by prejudice. Many thought we would be cutting across to Jericho, then up the Jordan. They never dreamed we would be going through Samaria. Those people turned back, although their numbers were few.

I was glad to see the dedication by those who saw Yeshua as more than just a novelty. They were consumed by His love and would follow Him to the end.

The road seemed like it was endlessly moving under my feet until dusk finally set on our weary heads. We made camp and settled in for the night. I went off by myself, for a short time, in order to process everything.

I leaned up against a tree and closed my eyes. It seemed like years had passed since my first encounter with this life; the two men who woke me... the friend I found in Simon. It was all so surreal. God had bestowed a gift on me that was beyond my thoughts or expectations.

How could I have lived my life on this planet without the knowledge of who The Messiah is? So many years wasted. I will have to make up for lost time. *My life is dedicated to you Father.* I thought of my family, and how they must be smiling down on me now. *I will see you soon... Sarah, Jake, Emily... I will see you soon.*

Chapter 12: Woman at the Well

"Wake up Lover… For we have slept through the morning. I'm sure your wife is wondering where you are."

The Samaritan woman rose from her bed and teasingly pulled the covers off the man who slept beside her.

"Get up my love!" She was met with cursing.

"Woman! Leave me be! I will sleep as long as I please! My head is aching, and my mouth is dry. Go fetch some water so that I may quench this thirst in me!" The man grabbed the blanket and yanked hard almost pulling the woman down with it. He pulled it over his head and rolled over.

"Have you not had your fill of me? Do *I* not quench your thirst?" she said in a playful tone of voice.

"You are nothing to me! Now go and get some water!"

A stinging pain shot through her heart. It seemed as though no man would ever see any value in her. It was her lot in life, she thought. To be loved by a man was unfathomable. She was dirty… worthless.

She saw his point and left for Jacobs Well to get some water. *Maybe when I return with water for his thirst and a plate of food, he will think better of me* she thought. All along her heart sank knowing that that would not be the case when she returned.

During mid-day, most people had already been to get water. In fact, she was usually back home before this time on most days. Too much wine and a very long night led to the basis of this unusual timing... or so she thought.

As she drew near to Jacobs well, she became hesitant to go any further. There was one lone man sitting there. He was a Jew. Normally she would wait until he left, but he was just sitting there... not drawing from the well. After a few moments, she realized he wasn't leaving any time soon. She had come this far and was determined not to leave without any water.

She decided to go to the opposite side from where he was sitting and draw from there. Jew, or not, he couldn't keep her from doing what she came to do. As she passed by him, she made sure not to make eye contact.

After reaching the opposite side, she began lowering the jar into the deep well. She soon felt the weight of the water as it filled the container and pulled the rope taunt. Carefully, she began drawing in the rope... keeping her eyes fixed on the pool of water below.

"Will you give me a drink of water?" The man's voice, though soft, startled her and made her jump. Never changing her gaze, she meekly answered.

"You are a Jew. How is it that you ask me... a Samaritan woman, to give you a drink?"

She finally raised her head enough to look at the man who spoke so kindly to her.

"If you knew the gift of God and who it is that asks you for a drink, you would have asked *Him,* and he would have given you *living* water."

"My Lord, you have nothing to draw water with and no rope to reach the depth of the well. Where can you get this living water?

Are you greater than our father Jacob, who gave us this well and drank from it himself, as did his sons… his flocks of sheep… and his herds of cattle?"

"Everyone who drinks from this well will be thirsty again, but whoever drinks the water that I provide for him will *never* thirst again. It will be a spring of water welling up inside him to eternal life!"

The Samaritan woman was somewhat confused, but yet certain that *she* wanted this water that he spoke of.

"My Lord, if it pleases you, give *me* this water so I won't be thirsty anymore, and have to keep coming here."

"Go. Go now to your husband and bring him back here."

She looked over her shoulder toward the city, then back at Yeshua. Sadness filled her voice as she said.

"I have no husband. I am not married."

"Yes… you are right to say you have no husband. The fact is, you have had *five* husbands, and the man you are now with is not your husband. What you have said is quite true."

She was startled at the revelation. How could he know about her secret life?

"I can see that you are a prophet. Please, tell me something. Our fathers worshiped on this mountain, but you Jews claim that the place where we must worship is in Jerusalem. Why?" Yeshua calmly answered.

"Believe me, woman, a time is coming when you will worship the father neither on this mountain nor in Jerusalem. You Samaritans worship what you do not know; we worship what we *do* know, for salvation is from the Jews. Yet a time is coming…" Yeshua paused and smiled, "…and has now come when true worshipers will worship the Father in spirit and truth, for they are the kind of worshipers the Father seeks. God is spirit, and his worshipers must worship in spirit and truth."

Many times during her life she had heard stories of one who would come and make things right. It was a story of hope and revelation. Her father once told her, in his last days alive, that a Messiah would come and that she must look for him.

Her father died when she was only seven years old. Her soul died with him. From that time on her life was filled with abuse, loneliness, and an unfulfilled life. No longer was she daddy's little girl, she was everyone's mat to step on; every man's soiled desire and the recipient of every woman's spiteful gaze. She was treated like a prostitute, yet she never sold herself for money, she gave of herself in the hope of being loved. Her past came flooding back and her emotions choked her voice out as she tried to speak.

"I kn…" She cleared her throat. "I know that Messiah is coming, and when he comes, *he* will explain everything to us!" Then to her surprised Yeshua said.

"I am the one you speak of." The woman's mouth fell open as the realization came to her.

"You? You… of course." She held her hands over her mouth and dropped the jar where she stood and ran down the road toward town jumping up and down, screaming with excitement. She ran by Simon and me, then pushed through the rest of the disciples and continued toward town at a dead run.

We all arrived to find Yeshua taking a drink from the jar that was left behind. Everyone was confused by the scene and cared not to ask what happened. John drew near to Yeshua and asked.

"Rabbi, we have food from town. Eat something." He held out a loaf of bread in offering to Yeshua, but he responded by saying.

"I have food to eat that you know nothing about."

The disciples muttered amongst themselves as to who could have brought him the food.

"My food is to do the will of him who sent me and to finish his work. Haven't you said before, 'four months more and then the harvest'? I tell you, open your eyes and look at the fields! They are ripe for the harvest. Even now the reaper is drawing his wages, and even now he is harvesting the crop for eternal life, so that the sower and the reaper may be glad together. So you see, the saying 'One sows and another reaps' is true. I sent you to reap what you have not worked for. Others have done the hard work, and you have reaped the benefits of their labor." Yeshua reminded them of the previous day's ministry. "Remember the harvest of souls that I left you with yesterday. Many are following me and are hearing my words. My words are being planted in their hearts. They will need harvesting. You must complete the work that I have begun."

Just then a crowd of people from the city arrived with the Samaritan woman leading them.

"See! Here is the man who told me everything I've ever done! Could this be The Messiah?"

The multitude of people gathered round and the level of noise increased as each person began to throw out questions. Peter stepped forward and addressed them with a booming voice.

"Please! Be quiet! If you want to hear from Yeshua, you must quiet down! Sit... Please!"

The crowd settled down and each found a place to sit and listen to the Messiah.

Yeshua spent a couple of hours sharing the love of the Father and The Kingdom with the Samaritans. Teaching from his heart and answering many questions. Many believed and begged him to stay on in Sychar for a while. As we started to make our way down the mountain, we were met with another group of people on their way up.

"Yeshua! Welcome back!" Psusennes yelled. "We heard the news that you were here and came immediately."

It was wonderful to see the change that had taken place in him in such a short time. He got rid of all his jewelry and his hair had grown back on his head, covering the tattoos that were so prominent before. He looked like a new man. I ran ahead to greet him.

"Psusennes! It is good to see you! You've changed!"

"Yes, my friend... Yeshua has changed my whole life!"

We embraced and he continued.

"We have heard many things about Jerusalem in the past week, and now you are all here again! Wonderful! Are you staying long? Please... you must stay awhile. Many things have been happening here as well. The testimony of Yeshua has spread throughout the city. We need someone here who can teach us. Many are seeking the Truth. Some of us have tried our best to explain Yeshua to them, but we need to know more. I am pleased you are all here."

Chapter 13: I Am Baal!

The square where Psusennes and I had met was a different scene than last time I came through here. The whole atmosphere was different.

Amazing! How could a city change that quickly from the work of one man?

Psusennes brought us to a group of people that seemed to be in authority... leaders of the community.

"You must be Benjamin! Psusennes has told us so much about you, and this Man of God. Please.... Sit with us."

I sat down and assessed the situation and began to speak.

"Thank you for..." I was interrupted by a distinguished gentleman... a *rich* man.

"Tell us, do you know this Yeshua personally?" His question was fraught with suspicion. "Do you believe him to be the Son of God?" His smile was crooked, and his eyes black like pools of deep, deep water. I couldn't help but notice the dried, white spittle crusted in the corners of his mouth. I didn't like the attitude that this man threw at me. I wondered why I was always the one who ended up facing the likes of men like this and not one of the other followers.

"Without a doubt! He IS the Son of God!" I yelled. "I find it interesting that, in spite of all the miracles, and all of the changed lives in this community, you question as to whether or not He is the

Son of God!" My blood was boiling a little bit. I had to calm down and present a more loving character than what was hiding beneath the surface. "*Yeshua... Help me*" I whispered. At that moment, a gentle hand rested on my shoulder.

"Benjamin, I think it best you step back for a moment." It was Yeshua. Without warning, a horrendous scream escaped the mouth of the rich man. He stood up and displayed an unusual persona. His body contorted unnaturally, and his face grew beat red with anger and rage. Psusennes and the others fell backward in horror, toppling over each other to get away from this Demon.

"*Why do you come here Son of God? Why do you take back what was given so freely to me so many years ago? The sacrifices of children and the sweet sounds of chaos have been ringing in my ears for centuries! This is MY territory! These are MY people!*" He hissed.

"What is your name?"

"*You know my name!*"

"Tell me your name!!"

"*I AM BAAL!!!*"

The personification of this demon was unlike anything I had ever seen before. I was stiff with fear... frozen in my tracks. I had faith that The Messiah could win this battle, but faith in myself... in front of such an awesome adversary? It had diminished to that of less than a mustard seed... to say the least. Yeshua stepped forward to meet Baal head on.

"Be gone Baal! Come out of him!"

The man's body shook with quakes, and jerks, and writhing. He fell on the ground and began rolling around, screaming in agony. Soon... he fell silent.

Yeshua knelt on the ground beside him and rested his hand on the man's forehead and seemed to be praying. The man opened his eyes and stared at Yeshua.

"What happened?" The rich man was in a state of shock. "I don't understand how I got here. Who are you?"

"I am Yeshua." With that declaration, there was no screaming, writhing, or evidence of any demonic activity. He was just serene and peaceful. "There are many changes that must be made in your life. You must stop the idol worship and sacrifices you have been doing. You have opened your heart up to Satan and his demons."

"But... this is all I have ever known! My father and his fathers have known and taught only this from the time of my birth. There is power and prestige that comes with it. Yet... I cannot deny the peace I have inside now. It's hard to explain it, but there is no heaviness now." A smile began to form on his face as he rose to his feet and embraced Yeshua. "Thank you for saving me Teacher! I want to know more of God and the life you bring!" I am Esdras.

Yeshua smiled and said, "Welcome to a new life Esdras."

Sychar was bursting with revival! Miracles were in abundance and lives were changed from hopelessness to a life of purpose. Leaders were chosen and trained in a short time to continue preaching The Kingdom to those who hadn't heard yet.

Next, we were on our way back to Galilee. First, to Nazareth, then on to Cana.

Chapter 14: The Nobleman's Son

"I'm sorry Jachin, there is nothing more we can do for the boy… It is out of our hands." The physician spoke rather curtly and with a dismissive tone to the father of the dying boy. He was the personal physician to King Herod Antipas. Why the King would command him to help a servant, albeit a nobleman, was beyond his comprehension. Frankly, even if he *could* the help boy, he wouldn't. He was thoroughly insulted that the King would lower his standards so much. He turned a cold shoulder to Jachin and quickly exited the room.

Nazareth was a waste of time. I was frustrated beyond belief! I aired my concerns with Simon.

"Yeshua was right! A Prophet has no honor in his own country! I thought He was being a little facetious stating that, but *WOW!* Those people were unbelievable!"

"I know!" Simon chimed in. "They would not listen to hardly a word He spoke. They only wanted miracles… Or to speak unkindly about Him! It was the complete opposite of Sychar! The Samaritans listened to every word He said, and they sought out the Truth more than the miracles!" Simon shook his head in disgust.

"Now I know why everyone keeps saying 'Can anything good ever come out of Nazareth?' No sir!" I shouted. "Nothing but Yeshua! He is the *ONLY* good thing about *this* place!"

Simon chuckled. "Ben... You must settle down! You do not see Yeshua all upset over it, do you? If anyone should be upset, it should be Him!"

"I know... You're right, of course." I was amazed at how much I have changed. Not long ago, I was just like the Nazarenes... Unbelieving, skeptical, and wanting tangible proof. Now I believe wholeheartedly in Yeshua. Not because of the miracles, but because of *WHO* He is. The changes He makes to the soul... far outweighs any miracles He may perform. I remember a conversation I had with Yeshua, just a few days ago.

"I am so hopeless!" Yeshua responded to my outburst with a comment.

"I am your hope."

"I am also so weak!"

"I *AM* your strength." Yeshua remained patient with me

"What am I going to do with my life?" I was having a real pity party.

"I have given you new life so you can live more abundantly."

We returned again to Cana where I had first met Yeshua. The atmosphere was not much different from that of Nazareth, for many there had seen or heard of the miracles performed in Jerusalem. They wanted the same... more miracles. As Yeshua was ministering in the courtyard of the city, a Nobleman and his entourage approached the gathering. He worked his way through the crowd and kneeled at the feet of Yeshua.

"Teacher! I beg of you... please come down to my home and heal my son. He is dying!" There were tears streaming down his face and the servants standing around him, looked on with great concern as he sobbed uncontrollably.

"Unless you people see signs and wonders, you will by no means believe." Yeshua was addressing the crowd here, then, turned his attention to the grief-stricken man. The Nobleman pleaded with Yeshua again.

"Sir, come down to my home before my child dies!"

Yeshua spoke to him with a smile on His face. "Go your way; your son lives."

Jachin rose from his feet and embraced Yeshua. There was no doubt in his eyes. He *KNEW* that his son was healed. He turned and started out in the direction from which he came. The following day, he was halfway home. A servant from his house was running toward him. As soon as he caught his breath, he exclaimed

"Master! It has happened! Aran is healed! He is well again!"

Jachin fell to his knees. "When did this happen?"

"Yesterday, about the seventh hour the fever left him, and he woke up!" Jachin realized it was the same time that Yeshua had declared him living. He now believed completely in Yeshua the Messiah and his whole household was converted too!

A few days had passed since the healing of the Nobleman's son. The crowd in the square was growing by the day. There were many people involved in what Yeshua taught, but there were also many on the outskirts of the crowd that were not interested in the Truth they were hearing. Their only interest was to disrupt and criticize. The day was waning, and the sun what sinking low. Yeshua was through with ministry and the crowd had slowly disappeared into the surrounding streets that connected to the courtyard. As we made our way back to our temporary quarters, we were accosted by some men of, shall we say… questionable character? They were homosexuals, and they were commenting on their particular interests in our group of men. Now I have always considered myself a "man's man", and to be acting in a feminine way is so far against my nature, that I found it repulsive to see these men acting in such a way. Two of these men approached Yeshua and expressed their interest in Him. We were all disgusted in the comments they were making and Peter, of course, made his way toward these men in order to physically shut them up when Yeshua stopped him.

"Peter. No, that is not the way." Yeshua turned toward the homosexuals to address them. One of them was obviously more outspoken than the other and stepped forward to meet Yeshua. The other stayed where he was. As he drew closer, it was obvious the he was wearing makeup, and his five o'clock shadow was beginning to bust through the paste he covered his face with.

"So, you are Yeshua. We have heard a lot about you these past few weeks." He spoke in a soft, womanly manner all the while using graceful hand gestures to exaggerate his feminine characteristics… as if to mock Yeshua and see what He would do. "Tell me… Do you find me attractive? Desirable? Most men do, but they won't let it be known. They just approach me in secret and keep their moral ineptitudes from their friends and family." I was ready to join Peter in pulverizing these two and sending them back to the side of the city they came from. Yeshua, just stared at him with compassion and spoke to his soul.

"You have never known real love, have you." That statement seemed to startle the man. "A long life of hurt and rejection, even as a child, has brought you to a place that you never thought possible."

"I have always been this way!" The womanly attributes seemed to vanish for a moment as he responded in anger. "You have no idea what I have been through. You don't know me… You don't know what I have been through!" It was obvious that Yeshua had struck a chord. This man was now shaking with emotion.

"I know that you were abandoned at a very young age and then exposed to things a child should never be exposed to. I know that the hurt you experienced is very deep, and very real." The man was tearing up now. He turned to find consolation in his partner, but his lover had gone and was nowhere to be seen now. "To be with a man is an abomination to God. He did not make you this way… man has. You must choose now, what life to live. I can tell you that God's love for you is real… It is complete, but you must repent of this lifestyle."

"But I know no other life! Has not God made me this way? I did not *choose* this life; it seems to have chosen me! However, what you have said is true. You must be the Son of God, because no one has ever known my past as a child. You could not have known unless you were sent from God. Still, how could God love me? I am the lowest of all sinners…. People detest me and make it a point to say so *daily*! I am not worthy of anyone's love or acceptance." He hung his head as tears streamed down his face. Being confronted with the truth began to break away the calluses that had formed over the years.

"Know this… I love you, as does God. I am in Him and He in me. Repent… turn from your sinful ways and begin a new life through me." At this, the man broke… uncontrollably sobbing, as he suddenly embraced Yeshua. We were all in shock, as we stood there, while Yeshua held this man as he cried. I didn't know what to think. In my time, homosexuality is mainstream. You can't watch a sitcom without seeing a gay couple on it. It is very much accepted by most in modern society. The Disciples were baffled. They were ready to stone this man, yet Yeshua is *embracing* him? Something really sunk in that day. I am so quick to judge someone for their *horrible* sins, thinking that their sin is worse than mine. Yeshua looks at *ALL* people the same and loves them all the same.

Chapter 15: Peter's Mother-in-law Healed

Nazareth, Galilee, and now Capernaum. Peter was excited to see his family again. It was said that we would stay here for some time… a kind of respite. When we reached Peter's home, there was an immediate sense of dread that hit us. Many remained outside, and even more on the outskirts of the city. Yeshua and some of us closest to Him made our way into the small home of Peter to find that his mother-in-law was deathly ill. She had contracted a fever and had not eaten or drank anything for three days. She was dying. Peter became quite distraught at first then pleaded with Yeshua.

"Yeshua! You must do something!" He was now cradling his mother-in-law in is arms. His eyes were wet with tears. The rest of his family who had been dealing with this the last couple of days were wailing. Peter cried "Please! You must heal her!"

Yeshua stepped forward and laid His hand on the side of peter's face. His eyes full of compassion and tearing up Himself as He saw the anguish in Peter's eyes.

"Peter… Your mother-in-law will be made well." Yeshua then knelt down and placing His hands on top of her head and spoke.

"Fever be gone! Rise up Mother."

The deathly ill woman opened her eyes as she quickly rose to her feet. Her fever was gone, and surprise was evident on her face.

"What happened? Last thing I remember was preparing fish for the evening meal." She was bewildered because of the look on every one's faces. Then she noticed Peter.

"PETER!" Her eyes were wide with excitement at the discovery of her son-in-law in her presence. "You are home!" She quickly embraced Peter. His eyes were moist with tears of joy now as he hugged her so tightly that I thought she would pass out again. Apparently, she was used to his strength and was so overcome with joy anyhow, that she was not fazed by his bear-hug. Peter's wife and children came running to his side now and hugs and kisses were in great supply.

As many times as I had read the scriptures, I never pictured the Disciples having any other life but that with Yeshua. They had truly sacrificed everything to follow Him.

It was refreshing to just experience the "home life" for a while. Traveling was grueling at times, and for the time being, many of the people following Yeshua dispersed and went their own way. Yeshua still ministered, and people still flocked to see Him, but it was a little more localized.

I had the privilege of staying with Andrew, and it was in his home that I met Hanna. Hanna was a cousin of Peter and Andrew. She had a sweet spirit and a great desire to know more about Yeshua. Andrew was very busy with things happening in his own family, so Hanna gravitated toward me with her questions. We spent hours upon hours discussing God's word and all the miracles that I had witnessed firsthand with Yeshua. It was during these discussions that I started noticing the sparkle in her eyes and the wisp of curly, jet black hair that always seemed to fall over one eye. For the first time in a long while, I was starting to even notice another woman. Sarah was the only woman I had ever been with. She was my first girlfriend, and my only love. I can never stop loving her, but my heart was finally ready to move on. I felt like a teenager again. I looked forward to seeing Hanna every day, and it was evident that she felt the same way too. Hanna was a widow. Her husband had died mysteriously, a few years earlier. They had only been married for a few months and she was left with no children. I could feel a bond developing between us, but there was a nagging feeling, beyond that bond, that said this could never happen. My time here was limited... I could feel it.

The Sabbath was upon us. Many were excited to know that Yeshua would be teaching in the Synagogue. A great crowd had gathered, and it was difficult to make our way inside the building. As Yeshua moved to the front and began to teach, I stood near the middle and noticed a man in front of me having a conversation with himself.

"No, I don't want to... I want to be free!" He was batting the sides of his head with his hands as if trying to swat at flies buzzing around him.

"Yes... You must, you must leave!" He shook his head violently. I was beginning to recognize this behavior and had a very bad vibe rolling up inside of me when all of a sudden, the man pushed his way through the crowd to the front.

"*Leave us alone*!" The wiry old man with filthy clothes and buggy eyes, screamed at Yeshua. "*Leave us alone! What have we to do with You, Yeshua of Nazareth*?"

His huge eyes began rolling back in his head to expose the white part, making him look even more grotesque and evil. He was twirling around like a dancer... bumping into people and flailing his hands about; hitting people in their faces. All of a sudden, he stopped dead in his tracks; his arms out to his sides, as if on a cross. His head was hung low. As he lifted his gaze slowly, he displayed a crooked grin on his face and began to laugh. His eyes weren't rolled back in his head anymore. I could see them now... black as pools of tar. I'd seen *that* look before. All of a sudden, the mocking smile was gone, and fear took its place as he stared down the Son of God.

"Did You come to destroy us? I know who You are... THE HOLY ONE OF GOD!" Yeshua starred back at him and then rebuked him.

"Be quiet and come out of him!"

The man's body contorted and twisted. Suddenly, he arched backward... violently, and began to float up in the air. People all around were frozen in disbelief as the body rose above their heads. Then there was a deafening scream and the body was hurled into the midst of the crowd; landing on top of a few men and breaking his fall. The crowd of men parted. The man was now on the floor looking up at the ceiling with a peaceful look on his face. Yeshua stepped up to him and offered his hand. The man took it and rose to meet his Savior.

"Yeshua! How can I ever thank you?" The man buried his face in Yeshua' shoulder and sobbed. "Thank you... thank you!"

A group of men next to me began to express their surprise at the event that unfolded right in front of them.

"What a word this is! For with great authority and power He commands the unclean spirits, and they come out!"

Word began to spread fast after *that* experience and many were seeking out Yeshua in great numbers again. Yeshua ministered throughout Galilee.

Chapter 16: Paralyzed in Sin

"Malchus! Please let us take you to him! He is over at the house of Cleophas. He is just around the corner. This is your chance!"

Malchus lay on his mat, tormented with feelings of hope and fear mingled together. For seven years now he has been a paralytic. After falling through a weak rooftop, he was never the same. Paralyzed from the chest down, he no longer had control of his life in *any* respect, except in what could be accomplished with his head. Thinking, talking, eating and breathing. Everything else was achieved through the help of his brothers and a few certain friends that had not yet abandoned him. His daily needs were met at the expense of others; helping him eat, cleaning up his bodily functions, keeping him company… and a multitude of other things. Now Yeshua was here. Malchus was torn. If anything, he desired to be healed so that his family and friends would be set free from having to care for him. Many times, he had wished death to come, but it evaded him. Such was his punishment. Many people had suffered financial loss due to his "cutting corners" in constructing homes for the lesser wealthy in the area. Ironic how his own shortcuts led to the demise he now suffered through. The roof he fell through was on one of his own buildings. He didn't deserve to be healed, but he could not bear the thought of these fine men sacrificing themselves for him in the years to come. He had to make a choice… undeserving or not.

"Take me to Him! I need to be healed!"

The men sprang into action, excited for their brother and friend; he *may walk today*… they all thought! Hurriedly, they affixed poles to his mat and began to carry him through the streets. As they rounded the corner, the scene was distressing. The crowd was so large, that men, women, and children were spilling out of the doorway and into the streets. People were straining to hear what Yeshua was saying. Malchus' brothers and friends conferred amongst themselves the options available and came to a conclusion. His brother shared the plan with him.

"Malchus…. The only way we can do this is to break a hole through the roof and lower you down to see Yeshua. It's the only way we can get around that mob. I know it will be difficult for you, but it must be done this way!"

Malchus stopped breathing for a moment and shut his eyes hard. The thought of being lowered through the roof brought back memories of the accident in vivid detail. Could he do this? He was scared to death! After what seemed like an eternity, he finally agreed to it. A narrow stairway, to the right of the house that Yeshua was in, led up to the roof. They could carefully lower him from the stairway and maneuver him on to the roof with little or no problem. Within five minutes they were in position and tools arrived quickly with the help of caring friends. The brothers worked frantically at breaking through the roof while the friends tied ropes to the four corners of the mat. They were now ready.

As Yeshua was speaking, a clump of ceiling fell from above; and the noise of digging was heard over head. Immediately, the people inside the house moved from the center of the room just in time to avoid the large section of building materials that crashed to the floor. Sunlight burst through the opening, revealing a cloud of fine dust and a mat being lowered by four ropes. When the mat settled on the floor, the ropes fell to the sides and four heads peered through the opening. People were in shock. What had just happened?

The paralytic on the mat looked as if he were dead. His eyes were transfixed and unmoving. Seeing this poor man lying on his mat, helpless, and unmoving, jogged a memory of my own paralysis after the accident.

"Benjamin?"

I heard a voice breaking through to my consciousness.

"Benjamin. Can you hear me?" My eyes opened to a stark white ceiling. "He's coming out of it. Ben, can you hear me? This is Dr. Washburn. You're at Mercy Medical in Rochester. You've been in an accident. You're going to be ok." I tried to move but was unsuccessful.

"Why can't I move?" It seemed my eyes were all I had control of.

"You were in a head on collision, You're banged up quite a bit. You suffered a severe concussion; in fact, we've had you in a drug induced coma for two weeks in order to give the swelling in your brain time to go down. You've also experienced numerous fractures. The reason you can't move is because of a temporary paralysis due to the swelling around your spinal cord. It will take a little more time to go away. This will dissipate and you should recover feeling in your extremities within a couple of days; although, it will still be a long road of recovery for you." As my thoughts began to clear, I was concerned for my family.

"Where's my family? Are they ok?" There was no answer... only silence.

"Please! How are my wife and kids?" Panic was rising up in me quickly. The Doctor turned to someone else in the room.

"Mrs. Messler, perhaps you should talk to Benjamin now. I'll leave you and the rest of your family alone."

"Thank you, Doctor Washburn." I could hear the door close behind him and saw my mother move into view.

"Mom! What's going on? How are Sarah and the kids? How bad are they? Please, tell me!" I could hear the heart monitor in the room beeping faster and thought my chest would explode. "Mother, please!"

"Ben..." My mother's voice trailed off as she tried to compose herself. "Benny, you need to rest, honey. Just get some rest and everything will be ok." There was an obvious reluctance in her voice. She was hiding something.

"Mom, how are Sarah and the kids?" She looked at me dabbing her eyes with a Kleenex.

"I'm so sorry Benjamin... they're gone."

"Gone? What do you mean gone? They *have* to be ok! They *can't* be gone!" My mind was playing back the accident and I was drawing a blank. All I could remember was the explosive crash and then waking up here in this room. At this point, Sarah's father Jim stepped forward and spoke up.

"Ben, I'm sorry, it's true. We lost Sarah and the kids. They died instan..." His voice trembled... he cleared his throat. "Instantly. They felt no pain." I could hear Sarah's mother in the room sobbing. My heart sank to a depth of pain I never knew could exist. *They are gone... Forever* I thought. *And I am left to live my life without them?* Anger welled up within me and a scream escaped me that was uncontrollable.

"GET OUT! GET OUT! ALL OF YOU! LEAVE ME ALONE!" I screamed at the top of my lungs. My mother recoiled in surprise and burst into tears. She cried out

"Ben, no! We won't leave you! You don't know what you're saying!"

I was blinded by anguish and unconcerned for her feelings at all.

"Get out!" I screamed. "I don't want to live! Pull the damn plug! Let me die! I want to die!" I started sobbing uncontrollably. Nurses burst in the door and called everyone back from the bedside.

"You need to calm down Mr. Messler! We are going to give you something." Within seconds, I felt the room slipping away as my family cried.

Yeshua knelt down beside him as the man blinked rapidly trying to remove the dust from his eyes. He finally focused on Yeshua. He was quiet for just a moment, and then tears started streaming down his cheeks, leaving a muddy trail. Malchus was held in a bondage of shame that was stronger than the weak shell of the body he was held prisoner in. He could escape his flesh through death, but his spirit was in danger, and he knew it... So did Yeshua.

"Son, your sins are forgiven you."

Murmuring was heard throughout the house. Some of the scribes were sitting there and reasoning in their hearts,

"Why does this Man speak blasphemies like this? Who can forgive sins but God alone?"

But immediately, when Yeshua perceived in His spirit that they were reasoning within themselves, He said to them.

"Why do you reason about these things in your hearts? Which is easier, to say to the paralytic, '*Your* sins are forgiven you,' or to say, 'Arise, take up your bed and walk'? So that you may know that the Son of Man has power on earth to forgive sins." He turned and said to the paralytic

"I say to you, arise, take up your bed, and go home!"

Immediately Malchus arose and gathered up his mat. At first, he just stood there; not able to comprehend that he was standing. He could feel the weight of his body on his legs and feet now. He could feel the texture of the mat that was rolled up in his hands. He could feel an ever so slight breeze wash over the hairs on his arms. Most of all though.... he couldn't feel the heaviness of his heart anymore. The dread of his past was gone, and a new feeling had emerged... it was love, peace and joy! He went out in the presence of them all jumping and shouting praises to God so that all were amazed and glorified God, saying,

"We never saw *anything* like this!"

Many of us watching were surprised at the lengths to which people would go through to reach Yeshua. In many instances, however, crowds became difficult to manage. At times it was necessary for Yeshua to just leave the scene; because of the mob mentality that would take over. When order dissipated and chaos ensued, ministry was next to impossible.

Chapter 17: Levi's True Wealth

Levi was awakened by the same dream again. The one where he is in a chamber full of gold coins stacked from floor to ceiling. As always, there was a feeling of euphoria. He loved gold. It was gratifying, stimulating, and so easy to come by. For him, as a tax collector, there was opportunity for a lifetime of wealth in his future. He didn't care that people despised him. He didn't care that he was making a profit from their misery; he only cared about his love of money. Gold was his idol, and being in, and amongst all of this shinning glory was overwhelming. Then, as always... the stacks of coins begin to fall; creating a landslide of heavy metal burying him alive. Pinned by the weight of the coins, he was unable to move; within minutes his face would be covered, and breathing was impossible. It was at this point he would wake up gasping for air. Levi lay there for a moment catching his breath. This dream had been reoccurring for at least a month now, and the bags under his eyes were proof of that! *How much longer must I suffer from this.*

Rising from his bed, he made his way to a basin and splashed water in his face. It was far from refreshing, but it was cooler than his sweat soaked bed clothes. It was times like this when he questioned his lot in life. When the gold and silver were not heavy in his hands and his eyes were not captivated by the beauty of it in the sunlight; here, in the dark, he was lonely. His greed had left him empty. His family, friends and wife had given up competing for his attention. The choice was his, and he had made it.

How foolish I have been, he thought... *to think that money could make me happy.*

For a brief moment, tears wet his eyes. He changed his clothes and made his way to work. Once again, feeling the weight of the money in his hands, he was fulfilled... for the moment.

After a full morning of ministry in Galilee, we made our way through the crowded streets of the city, bumping and sidestepping through the throng of midday traders. As we happened down a narrow side street, we stopped in front of a tax collector. He was sitting behind his table and looking at our group of people with shifty eyes and a cautious look; half expecting us to rob him or something. He was short, balding, and a little chubby. He wrung his hands anxiously as he stared up at Yeshua. Two rather large men stepped closer to him as if to show a presence of intimidation. Having this much money on hand was a dangerous business; by himself he would be unable to fend off any chance of robbery. We stood there waiting and wondering what Yeshua was doing. Finally, he spoke directly to the tax collector

"Follow me."

It was a short, simple statement... yet apparently effective in bringing this man to action. The tax collector turned and spoke quietly to one of his men, then moved around his table to face Yeshua.

"Please, come and eat. I have plenty of food and drink for you and your men" He gestured with his hands, "Would you honor me by accompanying me to my home?"

In the crowd of people, that were always following Yeshua, certain scribes and Pharisees felt it their duty to discredit Him when possible... this was one of those times.

By the time we reached Levi's house, word had already spread about our dinner date. A small, but noisy crowd had gathered outside the gates of Levi's home to criticize Yeshua for eating at a tax collectors house. In Jewish tradition, eating with someone was an intimate act. This was considered just a step below the intimacy of marriage; so you can imagine the shock of everyone, including the disciples. Nathaniel, who was usually one for stretching the limits... was unusually grieved. Nathaniel happened to be walking beside me, so I was the one to receive his take on the subject.

"Why *are* we coming here? I understand Yeshua sharing the truth with this man out on the streets, but *eating* with him... in his home?" His face was red.

"Calm down Nathaniel" I said, "Do you remember what I told you about the inn in Sychar; and how He spoke to the drunkards and prostitutes? Don't forget what Yeshua has taught us. We cannot judge Levi for what he does. He still needs to hear the truth, and if it means eating with him in his home and showing him love... we must do it." Nathaniel lowered his head in shame; and pushed aside his prejudice.

"You are right Benjamin. I have been willing to accept the things I'm comfortable with, but this *one thing* is difficult for me! My father was thrown into a debtor's prison for some time because of a tax collector. This man was adding on extra taxes for his own profit!"

"I am sorry Nathaniel. I can understand why you feel this way."

"Thank you, Benjamin for helping me to see my own sin in this matter." He allowed a slight smile to form on his lips.

As we entered through the gates and into the courtyard, I was taken aback back by the ornamental garden, statues and, well... stuff. If a bachelor pad could be expressed in a picture... this was it! It was gaudy! He definitely needed a woman's touch on the place.

Some of Levi's business acquaintances started to arrive; having been invited ahead of time by Levi's bodyguard. There were tax collectors and sinners, and sinners and tax collectors. It was an elite group to say the least. In the wake of the new arrivals, it didn't take long for Levi's servants to whip up a *glorious* feast. We all sat down to eat. When Peter saw the plethora of food arriving, his stomach took over and the frown he was carrying, disappeared from his face. The way to a man's heart is through his stomach... or so they say.

When all had eaten their fill, Levi began to tell the account of his reoccurring dream. He was obviously very troubled by it. He spoke directly to Yeshua now.

"Yeshua, some say that You are a prophet... can you tell me what my dream means?"

"Levi, God wrote the Laws of Moses on stone, but he *also* wrote the Law on your heart as well. Do you not know the answer to your question already? If you search within the depths of your heart, you would know that you have made money your idol. The scriptures read that 'you are to have no other Gods before Me.' I think now, you are beginning to understand that gold cannot satisfy you no matter how much you have in your storehouses." Yeshua looked at Levi with great compassion "In the end, you will reap death, but if you follow Me, you will have life eternal."

After *that* statement, all of the other tax collectors that were present, derided Yeshua, gathered together, and left Levi's home.

None other than Levi and a few others remained. They still wanted change in their lives.

"Yeshua" cried Levi, "We want to be free from our bondage. I can't speak for the rest, but *I* will follow you!" Levi turned and motioned to his belongings. "I will sell everything; give back the money that I overcharged for taxes... then the rest I will give to you. Will you have me Yeshua? Can I follow you?"

I was amazed at the stark change in Levi; to give up such wealth, *had* to be difficult. Yeshua then did something unexpected.

"Levi, from this moment on, you will be known as Matthew."

Chapter 18: The Sheep Gate

Elah opened his eyes for the hundredth time only to be greeted by darkness once again. The sun's rays had not yet painted the eastern sky and the roosters had not yet crowed. He would wait for *that*. When the rooster crows, he would begin his morning commute. For a moment, he was doubtful. *Why bother? Twelve years, and every attempt has been in vain!* For years now he has made his morning trek to the Gate of Arman; the Sheep Gate… also known as the Pool of Bethesda. Would this day be any different? The cock crowed… his heart responded as if it were called into battle; he had feelings of excitement, anxiety and fear. Somehow, today seemed different. It was as if destiny may finally see *him* in the waters today when it is stirred by the unseen hand.

Rolling off his mat, Elah sat up. He stared at his lifeless, child-like limbs. His whole life, of thirty-eight years, have been for the most part… good. His family has shown great support and have provided for all of his needs except his independence. He so desired to be on his own; to have a job, a wife, and even children. His handicap had prevented all that. Five years ago, he started going to the Pool of Bethesda in order to seek out healing. He was tired of being alone and having no one to share his life with – his dreams. Many times, he would see happy couples walking together and wishing he could do the same. He was a handsome man. Many times, women would take notice of him; but as soon as the covering was removed from his legs, they would look away and simply disappear.

He quietly rolled up his mat and linen and strapped it to his shoulders. After thirty-eight years of dealing with his infirmity, he could get around on his own quite well. However, it was slow going at times. Glancing over at his sleeping parents, he longed to see their burden lifted. They never complained, and they had loved him through everything imaginable. He hoped that today, he would beat everyone into the pool. He *had* to do it! Elah began his journey. His calloused knuckles, thick from years of moving about, supported his frame instead of strong legs and broad feet. His arms and upper torso would flex with each stride he took, showing his musculature and strong development over the years. The sound of wood, strapped to his useless legs for protection, would scrape the ground; making a familiar echo in the narrow streets that most had come to recognize as the cripple. It was sad to think that the thousands of attempts at being first to dip in the pool, were often beat out by someone else who was one one-hundredths of a second faster; and that was *only* if he could get a seat close to the waters. Many days, he was far from it.

Rounding the last corner, Elah's heart sank. With the Feast of the Jews going on, there were more people in Jerusalem... and that meant more sick people searching for healing. Out of the five porches surrounding the water, there were few places left, and none right beside the pool that he could get to. Most had arrived in the evening and slept in their place over night. As he was pondering whether to stay or turn home, a man stumbled over his legs and hit the ground cursing. As he got up, he yelled in frustration.

"Every year, I come to this *same* gate! And every year I have to find my way through all of these bodies! Why do I keep taking this same passage when there are other gates to choose from!" He looked at Elah and softened. "Please forgive me. My words are not meant for you or these other less fortunate souls. I curse myself for not looking where I was going! Are you hurt? Elah had no feeling in his legs, so he was unsure. He reached down to feel his limbs with his hands and searched with his eyes and found no sign of injury.

"I am whole. I believe nothing is injured." The man smiled with relief and offered his services in apology.

"May I help you to a better place at the pool?" Elah was shocked at the man's hospitality and could only nod his thanks. The kind man then lifted him up and carefully stepped through the maze of bodies. Finding one of the last available openings, he sat him down and quickly left before Elah could thank him. *If only he could have stayed to help me get in the pool when the water stirs,* he thought.

It has been almost a full year since we started following Yeshua. Watching Simon grow in the faith and knowledge of Yeshua The Messiah, and finding myself and my world turned upside down, has been nothing short of a miracle. The world I left behind seemed more and more like a dream, and *this* world my reality. The Benjamin Messler from Pennsylvania no longer existed, although everything I learned in that time has been, in a sense, fulfilled... more meaningful. All of the teachings and all of the study have brought it to fruition. It was preparation for what I was now experiencing. The thought of going back saddened me, but I knew in my heart that my time here was short.

After a long restful winter in Capernaum, it was nice to be traveling again. We were only a couple of hours away from Jerusalem now... headed there for another Passover. As we began to interact with more people again, it was obvious that there was a noticeable change in the way the crowds received Yeshua now. Many still sought him out for his teaching and healings, but many were also out to disprove him. There were those who desired a King to take over the Jews and overrun the Roman influence here, and still others who sought to condemn him and see him brought to ruin.

With the Mount of Olives to our back, we entered the Northeastern Gate of the city, which was known as the *Sheep's Gate*. Crowds of people traveling on the main road began to back up in clusters and then bottleneck in order to get through the gate. Finally, after two hours of inching forward, we were through. Just inside the gate were vendors and money changers. We all bought something to eat and then proceeded to the right, following Yeshua. The first site of significance after entering Jerusalem was the Pool of Bethesda. It was packed with week and torn lives… people whose spirits had been crushed by disease and handicaps. It saddened my heart to see so many so destitute. Yeshua turned toward them and the rest of us followed. We carefully stepped our way over people in order to get closer to the pool and were cursed by those waiting for the pool to stir. Yeshua stopped before a man who was crippled, sitting on a mat. Yeshua just stood there, looking at him. The man looked up at Yeshua and toward the rest of us gathering around. Yeshua didn't speak. He just looked at the man. The cripple began to feel a little uneasy and started fidgeting a little. Yeshua was the first to speak.

"Do you want to be made well?" The man looked shocked. He kind of smiled as if to *get the joke* and laugh along but was obviously hurt over the question asked of him.

"Sir, I have no one to help me in the pool when it is stirred, up; but while I am moving toward it, another steps down before me. Yeshua looked at him and calmly spoke.

"Take up your bed and walk."

Elah strained his ear toward Yeshua as if to get a repeat of what he said when all of a sudden, he heard the straps that held the wood on to his legs snap. His legs jerked uncontrollably which forced him to fall on to his back. The linen covering his legs shuttered violently and his feet began to inch out past the hem of cloth. He felt a hot sensation burning through his body as strength returned to his limbs... a feeling he had never known before. He sat up and removed the linen from his legs and gasped in amazement. His legs were no longer childlike, but those of a full-grown man! Elah scramble to his feet. He felt as if he were eight feet tall! He was standing eye to eye with Yeshua... something he had never experienced before. He just wavered there, dumbfounded. Others sitting around started shouting and screaming to be next. Yeshua smiled at Elah as he struggled to keep his balance. Elah kneeled down and rolled up his mat and did what Yeshua commanded and carefully stepped through the crowd of crippled and lame people. They continued screaming to be healed and groped at Elah as if by touching *him*, they could be healed. As he made his way out of the courtyard, there were a certain few Jews standing there with disgust on their faces. One of them spoke their concerns.

"You there! This is The Sabbath! It is not lawful to carry your mat!" Elah wasn't sure what to say.

"A man at the pool did this. I don't know who he is. He just told me to 'Rise, take up your mat and walk'. My legs became strong again. I rolled up my mat and I am as you see me here! I am going to the temple now to thank God for my healing!" Elah looked the men dead in the eyes and threw the bed at their feet. "You may have this... I don't need it anymore!" Elah smiled and walked with a spring in his step toward the temple.

As Elah made his way through the streets, he began to think of all the things he can do now; work a real job, become independent. His thoughts then strayed to all the parties he had with his so-called friends. It was a common thing for them to get him drunk and have woman force themselves on him, knowing that he could not act in the sense of a real man. They would all laugh, and he would join in the laughter while dying of hurt inside. He was always allowed at the parties for entertainment. His heart sank then became vengeful. *I will show them* he thought. Suddenly, a sharp pain shot through his legs! He stopped, bent over and rubbed his legs for a moment. *"Not used to this yet, are you, legs?"* he thought. His mind strayed back to his thoughts before the pain came. He was better looking than all of his friends, but never had the lower half of his body to be a complete man. Now he was complete and could do some things he had never done before. As he worked his way through the maze of streets, he happened past his friends' local hangout. There were the regular prostitutes outside selling their wares and they looked on in shock as he approached them – the very ones that had taunted him in the past.

"Hello Elah!" They cooed. "What has happened to you?" The three woman surrounded him and began caressing his face and grabbing at him. "Now that you are a whole man, maybe we can have a little more fun together." They all laughed. Elah's anger burned inside him, yet he was feeling lust in his body like he had never known before! He broke away from them.

"Not now!" I am on my way to the temple to thank God for my healing. Please let go of me!"

The women stepped back as if hit by an electrical shock that soon wore off. They started laughing again as one said.

"Well pray for *US* when you get there!"

They stepped away, giggling, and began their normal sales pitch to the others walking by. Elah began to feel more relaxed again as he neared the temple. As he reached the top of the steps, a familiar face waited there... the man that had healed him. Elah approached him.

"Who are you, a prophet?" Elah questioned. Yeshua smiled, but then looked concerned.

"I am Yeshua. See... you have been made well. Sin no more, lest a worse thing come upon you." Elah was caught off guard. Did this Yeshua know what he had been thinking just moments ago? Never-the-less, he would obey. He would not live his life like he had in the past. This was a new lease on life, and he intended to spend the rest of his life praising God for his healing!

"Thank you Yeshua, I will give thanks to God and repent of my ways! I feel clean and renewed. I do not want to go back to my life before!"

Yeshua smiled as Elah made his way into the temple and showed himself to the priests. As he approached the priests, shock was evident on one of their faces.

"Elah! It can't be... You are walking?" The priest was beside himself with wonder. He had known Elah from childhood, and to see him now, was hard to fathom.

"Priests... I have come to show myself and give praise to God, for I have been healed!"

"Elah, how did this happen?" The priest showed a tinge of happiness for Elah at first, but soon turned skeptical. He had heard the stories of Yeshua and was not happy about the turmoil that was being caused by this heretic. "Elah, please tell us... who did this to you?"

"I was at the Pool of Bethesda, waiting for the water to stir as I always do, and a man approached me and asked me if I wanted to be well. For years I have been going there and no one has ever helped me into the pool... I was hopeless. Now here stood a man asking me if I want to be well? Before I could answer him, he said 'take up your bed and walk'. My legs began to shake and become strong again. I stood up, picked up my mat, and here I STAND before you now! I am healed!"

The grin on his face was hard to contain but scowls quickly formed on the mouths of the priests. One screamed out his response in boiling anger, almost knocking the young man over with its force.

"WHO WAS THIS MAN? WHO DID THIS TO YOU?"

Elah stepped back and wiped the spittle deposited on his face from the angry priest. He timidly answered

"It was Yeshua... He said his name was Yeshua."

The priests went into action, spinning around and heading further into the Temple at almost at a dead run toward the High Priest. Elah stood there motionless.

Chapter 19: The Trap

The priests met in secret to devise a plan that could be carried out quickly. The High Priest took charge of the meeting.

"Elzaphan.... Is not your servant's son crippled? Does he not have a hand that is withered? Go! Bring him here so that we may catch this Yeshua healing on the Sabbath! We will then have evidence against him. The people cannot dispute it!"

Elzaphan rushed out of the chamber to get his servant's son while the remaining priests set out to find Yeshua and corner him.

Elzaphan's bait was in place as Yeshua walked through the corridor. He walked directly up to the man with the withered hand as if prompted by a script. The priests stood close by and watched as Yeshua did nothing. The High Priest then spoke with arrogance so thick, it made it difficult for some to breathe as they awaited the outcome of this ambush.

"Is it lawful to heal on the Sabbath?"

Yeshua looked up at the High Priest in order to face His accuser.

"What man is there among you who has one sheep, and if it falls into a pit on the Sabbath, will not lay hold of it and lift it out?

Of how much more value then, is a man than a sheep? Therefore, it is lawful to do good on the Sabbath." He turned back to the crippled man.

"Stretch out your hand."

The man stretched out his hand and everyone was amazed. It was completely whole. In shock the young man held out his other hand to make a comparison...holding them side by side, turning them over and back again. He was speechless... and so were the priests, aside from the sounds of their guttural discontentment. There was no mercy in the hearts of these men. They left in a hurry and began to plot and scheme to destroy this Nazarene.

Ever since Simon and I started following Yeshua, it became evident that things were going to change dramatically. Each day held new surprises. Simon turned to me and commented on the situation.

"What do you think Benjamin? Do you think it wrong that Yeshua has healed so many on the Sabbath? This is hard for me to understand. Even after all this time of following Yeshua, I still find things strange. I am not accustomed to certain things under The Law... changing. This is difficult." Simon was clearly torn between The Law, and this new Gospel that Yeshua was bringing to the Jews.

"What does your heart tell you Simon? The Law was set up to show us ourselves, and how impossible it is to follow it perfectly. That is why God provided a way out through sacrifices. We are incapable of being perfect. Besides, how many of the laws that you follow were made up by man and not God? They took something such as the Sabbath, that God ordained, and added their own laws to it. Yeshua has very plainly shown the difference in the two."

"Yes, I see that what you say is true. However, it is still difficult to overcome all that I have learned since I was a small child."

I understood exactly how Simon felt. I spent my youth learning the same things, but my studies, later in life, took me into the New Testament as well. I now can see firsthand how all this is playing out. It all made sense to me now.

Chapter 20: The Imposter's Pulpit

Following the Sabbath miracles, we stayed around Jerusalem for a short time. At one point, Simon and I struck out on our own one afternoon to buy some supplies. As we made our way through the narrow streets, we heard a commotion up ahead. At first, we thought we had stumbled upon Yeshua healing or teaching in this part of the city. As we drew closer, it was quite evident that it was not. People were practically trying to climb over each other to get to the front of the crowd that had gathered in the small square. I asked a bystander what was happening. He stood there observing, but not engaged like the others were.

"What is going on up there?"

The man turned briefly enough to see who it was that was speaking, and to clarify if he was the one being spoken to, then calmly turned his attention back to the excitement.

"I am told that Yeshua is up there healing." Then he added "For a small price."

Simon and I looked at each other is disbelief.

"Are you saying that Yeshua is asking to be paid for these healings?"

Before I could get the last word out of my mouth, someone in front of us dropped a handful of coins that scattered under the feet of those around him. People clamored for the money and left him standing there, dumbfounded, and unsure as to what to do now. Simon got red in the face, grabbed my arm, and proceeded to push our way through the throng of people to the front.

"This cannot be! Come… We must find out who this is!"

A portly gentleman was speaking in front of the people. He was side by side with about six other men who were keeping the crowd at bay and collecting the money. The large fellow bellowed to the crowd. He sounded like an infomercial.

"Stand clear! I beg you to stop pushing! You need healing? Deliverance? Wealth? You will all get a chance to see Yeshua for your need! The price has been set, and you WILL not see him unless you pay first!"

I was livid now. How dare they, first of all, claim to have Yeshua up there, and second of all, charge for his services???

This false *Messiah* was standing behind his entourage, *ministering* to someone. He spoke to his supporter in an authoritative voice.

"What is it that you desire from God?" He placed his hands on the man's shoulders and looked directly in his eyes. The man answered with excitement and hope in his voice.

"I have need of healing. They say my left eye will never have sight again."

"Yes… Yes, I see that your eye is clouded." He sounded so concerned.

"Also, I want more wealth. I am a businessman and I am in need of more money."

"WAIT!" The portly man shouted out in anger to the man. "You only paid for the miracle, not for the wealth! If you want more wealth, you have to pay more money!"

Two of the other men grabbed the poor fellow and began to escort him away.

"I can pay more!" The men relaxed their grip and he reached into his purse and pulled out two more coins. "Is this enough?" The two men let go of him and one of them snatched up his purse, leaving him holding the two coins between his fingers.

"That should be sufficient for your request." The heavy-set man gave him a crooked smile and turned back toward the crowd and continued selling. The false *Messiah* proceeded once the correct price had been paid.

"Do you trust me young man? You have to trust me if you want these things."

"Yes." The gullible man closed his eyes. "I believe."

This so-called Yeshua looked up to heaven and prayed a generic prayer to bless him. What happened next, I could not believe. The false healer drew back his arm and then punched the young man in the eye. The crowd gasped and the man doubled over in pain, covering his eye with both hands. He looked up briefly in anger then softened into a state of confusion.

"The things of God are far above our understanding!" The healer spoke to the crowd then turned his attention back to the man with the swollen eye. When the swelling goes down .... You shall see again!"

The crowd cheered, apparently liking the show that was being played out before them. The beaten man walked away unsure of his future outcome, yet too stunned by it all to raise a fuss. I'd seen the same on television when I was bored and channel surfing. The faith healer gets the crowd all worked up and the crowd blindly follows their smooth talking and hypnotic charisma. Experts say that in order to tell the difference between a counterfeit bill and a real one is to become familiar with the real thing first. Well, I had experienced the real thing, and it was *real* easy to spot the fake ones now. Simon and I found our voices above the noise of the crowd.

"He is NOT The Messiah! He is not Yeshua! This man is NOT Yeshua The Messiah!"

The mass of people quieted their excitement for about a second, and then began hurling insults at us as *Yeshua's* faithful associates began hurling fists our direction. The blunt, repeated force began to darken my vision and the ground was soon hitting the back of my head! Then the ribs cracked as dusty feet began pummeling my sides and body! The last thing I remember was the scrapping of my face as my body was being dragged away from the altar of falsehoods.

I awoke to the sound of children laughing and made an attempt to move. I hadn't felt this physically damaged since my accident. There was pain in so many places on my body that I couldn't pin-point any one spot that hurt more than the other. Simon was lying propped up against the wall beside me and groaning. I had sand in my eyes. I leaned over, blinking fast, trying to tear up so as to wash the gritty substance from my vision. Simon's eyes were all but swollen shut from the beating, and he had a fat lip so big, I thought his skin would burst. He tried to speak but found it too difficult. He carefully laid his head back and rested it on the wall behind him; content to just leave the moment unspoken. We sat in silence as people walked by staring, but not too concerned with our appearance.

"Benjamin! Simon! We have been looking everywhere for you!" Nathaniel and a few other men knelt beside us to examine the extent of our wounds then proceeded to help us up and then back to the rest of our group.

I had one man on each side of me, carefully supporting me as we made our way through the crowd toward Yeshua. Simon was being carried now. His wounds were more extensive. As I glanced at him, the seriousness of his wounds were made clearer. Parts of his clothing were literally soaked with blood. He was in bad shape. At some point along the way back, he had passed out.

Yeshua noticed our approach and met us halfway. My cohorts gently eased me to the ground next to Simon just as Yeshua came along side us. Concern turned to a smile as we made eye contact.

"Well Benjamin, looks as if you found yourself some trouble."

His voice was so calming, and his humor lightened my worried spirit. Yeshua would fix things... I believed it with all my heart. Yeshua took hold of Simons hand and prayed in silence. Before my eyes, the blood-soaked clothing began to dissipate. The swelling around his eyes and mouth began to go down, and his dark bruising turned to a nicely, flesh colored skin again. Simon took in a sharp quick breath and opened his eyes as he sat up straight. He looked around, not sure of where he was, or what had happened. When he saw me, he nearly jumped out of his skin.

"Benjamin! You look as if death has taken you!" Yeshua put a hand on his shoulder and Simon relaxed a bit.

"He will not die... just believe,"

He smiled, reassured that Yeshua meant what he said. Yeshua then turned to me and laid His hands on my head. As He prayed, warmth entered my body. It increased with an intensity that I thought would burn me up; but instead it quickly salvaged every tissue fiber and every bone that was compromised by the beating I took. Within seconds, I felt whole once more. I had now been delivered from demons, saved from an eternal damnation, and now physically healed from a pretty good whooping! Yeshua turned to the astonished crowd, and then addressed us all with a warning.

"Watch out that no one deceives you. For many will come in My name, saying 'I am The Messiah,' and will deceive many. Benjamin. Simon. You have been faithful to the Father and to Me. Thank you."

Yeshua grabbed both of our hands and pulled us up to a standing position. I felt good... real good! Simon and I embraced each other. Then, as I turned back to look at Yeshua, I caught the stare of someone behind Him who I hadn't really paid attention to until now. His gaze was fixed on Yeshua. He had a smile on his face, but it was somehow wrong. The eyes were dark and void of any joy. In fact, they were lifeless pools of darkness, and the smile on his face was somewhat twisted into a half scorn. His eyes never left Yeshua. Immediately, I felt a shiver go up my spine. This was Judas Iscariot!

Chapter 21: Judas Iscariot

Judas had always seemed to collect trouble, and this day was no different. His father was seething with anger!

"Judas! Judas! Come here boy!"

Judas knew better than to drag his feet, so he quickly presented himself to his father. The moment he stepped in front of him, he was met with a stinging backhand.

"I told you to help your mother while I was gone! Now, I come back to find you haven't lifted a finger to do the tasks I left you with!" He grabbed Judas by the nap of hair on the back of his neck … pulling hard and bringing tears to his eyes. He then led his boy like a dog to door of the house and proceeded to toss him through it like a rag doll! Judas landed on his face in the dirt. He gradually regained his strength and pulled himself up to his hands and knees. "Don't come back here you worthless pig of a son! We are better off without you eating up our food and lying around all day long! Go!" Judas's father stepped forward and brought his foot up, hard into the stomach of his only son. Judas felt the immense pain of rejection more than the physical one that took away his breath.

Judas had always wanted to please his father but found his life with his friends to be more fulfilling. They thought of *him* as s*omebody*, and always looked up to him. He would usually entertain them by crossing a line that they were too afraid to cross themselves. Why should he do a mindless, unfulfilling chore, when he could receive praise, and pats on his back for stealing something... fighting someone... or telling a grand tale of adventure that his friends would unwittingly believe. He was on his own now.

Just one more thing to impress his friends. He thought.

First order of business would be to find a place to stay. His friend's parents would never allow him to stay with them. They knew his type, and didn't want *their* precious children playing with him, but his friends did it just the same. The only other option he had was to find Elzaphan, the priest. He had done a few errands for him in the past and had always shown a liking to Judas. Perhaps he could do more for him now that his time had been freed up significantly. He would enjoy hanging around all the politics and things the priests did in secret. This had always appealed to him. Now it may become an everyday thing... yes, life was getting better!

Judas spent most of his teenage years with the priest, doing exactly what he thought he would... running errands, learning about politics and the Priesthood, and most importantly, how to use situations to his own benefit. He was on his own now and had perfected his art. Stealing things outright was child's-play! He was now seasoned enough to operate in more subtle manners of theft. Politically, he knew the right buttons to push for each party of government for the furtherance of his own profit. Spiritually, he could hold a religious debate with the best of them. This is why conversation around the city would prick up his ears so often. News had spread about a man named Yeshua. This man was gaining momentum in his following. Hundreds were flocking to see and hear Him. Money was practically being thrown at Him. There was prestige and profit to be had and he wanted in on the action.

Yeshua was preaching in the city of Kerioth, south of Hebron one morning. It was cool, and the marketplace was bustling with commerce as people began their day. The air was filled with the smell of fresh herbs, spices, and bread. Judas was standing at the back of the crowd observing Yeshua. Watching how He interacted with the multitude and how they responded was, to say the least, intoxicating! Judas was smitten with the whole ordeal, yet a side of him was intrigued with this man called Yeshua. Judas had never trusted anyone at their word, but *this* man was somehow different. He spoke with authority and He seemed to genuinely care about these people. There was evidence of compassion that was so very foreign to Judas. As a man now nineteen years of age, Judas had seen more in his life than most men had at thirty. One thing he had never encountered before was love. He'd heard about it but had never experienced it firsthand.

Judas physically shook his head in an effort to empty out the feelings that came over him. Cold and calculating, were actions that were familiar to him; this experience was not. The wheels started turning again as he focused his attention back on the scene in front of him. Yeshua was gone… Where did He go?

"Have you considered My words? Have you seen the healings? Why are you here, Judas?"

Yeshua stood there… quiet. It felt as if He were looking at his very soul. Could He see it? Could He know his true heart? *Wait! How does He know my name?*

"How do you know me, teacher? Yes, I have considered Your words and seen the healings, but I know not what I should do."

"I know what My Father has told Me. Will you join me Judas? Will you follow Me?"

Judas found himself shaking his head *yes*, and began a journey wrought with hope, fear, truth, lies… and ultimately, tragedy. In one facet, he found his place as the treasurer and as a disciple of Yeshua the Messiah. In another – he was torn in his heart and mind, continually. Greed, and the desire to be accepted, would be a power-play throughout his time with The Messiah.

Chapter 22: The Twelve Are Called

Once outside the city, it seemed like things died down a bit. There were still the throngs of people seeking out Yeshua, but the hectic *city* life was no longer a hindrance to it. Out here we had space and fresh air. I found it exhilarating. As dusk showed its last rays of sunlight, I was reminded of the night before I went with Simon to Cana and the sunset over the olive trees. It was a bit warmer on this evening, but nonetheless just as beautiful. The peace that I had in my heart was different now than it was then too. I have met Yeshua, heard His teachings, and have seen the miracles. How could my life not be changed? Yeshua was all I could ever hope for and more.

Simon, who was sitting nearby, stirred from his own thoughts as he noticed some movement near a grove of trees.

"There goes Yeshua... off to pray again. Does He ever sleep?" He shook his head in disbelief. "I could not do it. I am tired beyond belief. I could not see myself praying all night, only to be met with a full day of crowds chasing me down in the morning." He yawned and stretched out prone in the attempt to sleep.

"I agree brother... I could not do it either, but He gets His strength from God and keeps going."

I too felt exhausted as I settled in for the night. Tomorrow would be a good day. I fell asleep with a smile on my face.

The next morning, we were shook awake by Nathaniel.

"Come. Yeshua has called everyone together."

Simon and I stretched out the kinks and followed Nathaniel over to a sort of flat terrain on the side of the mountain. Yeshua was there waiting patiently while talking to Peter and John. There were about a hundred of us gathered as we formed a half circle around Yeshua. Some who gathered, were still half asleep, while others were more awake and anxiously awaiting word from Yeshua. Simon of course was one of the perky ones. Morning was his time. Morning was *not* mine, but I was still was anxious to hear what this was all about. Yeshua stood on the hillside a little above the plateau we were on, so everyone could hear Him.

"The Father has shown me that I am to pick out twelve among you to be apostles. You are to be sent out with authority and to share my message."

The look on Peters face was evident. It looked the same way when Yeshua asked us to baptize people. Yeshua continued as He looked directly at Peter.

"Peter, do not fear what I ask of you. You have learned much from Me. You *HAVE* authority, and you will teach My message to the lost sheep of Israel. You will be able to heal, and to cast out demons in My Name. Simon Peter… come forward."

He then turned His attention to the rest of us and gazed through the crowd, searching. As he made eye contact with the ones who were to be chosen. He called them out to Him.

"Andrew, James and John… come. Philip and Bartholomew, Matthew and Thomas. Come here with Me. James, son of Alphaeus. Also, you… Simon the Zealot. Judas, son of James come forward."

When Judas' name was called, I turned again to the realization that he would betray Yeshua. It was hard to comprehend how

God would choose such a vile creature, but yet, His will must be accomplished. As much as I wanted to yell out *IMPOSTER*! My mouth remained closed. Judas seemed almost as shocked as I was. He quickly moved into his place of authority and smirked as if he had just gotten away with something. I knew it wasn't right, but I wished, at that moment, that I could kill Judas Iscariot.

After the twelve were selected, Yeshua had us all sit down before the Disciples left and shared one last Word with them.

"These things you must know and comprehend before you go out. Remember these words and apply them to your life." Yeshua closed His eyes and seemed to pray for a moment, then continued.

"Blessed *are* the poor in spirit, for theirs is the kingdom of heaven. Blessed *are* those who grieve, for they shall be comforted. Blessed *are* the humble, for they shall inherit the earth. Blessed *are* those who hunger and thirst for righteousness, for they shall be filled. Blessed *are* the merciful, for they shall obtain mercy. Blessed *are* the pure in heart, for they shall see God. Blessed *are* the peacemakers, for they shall be called sons of God. Blessed *are* those who are persecuted for righteousness' sake, for theirs is the kingdom of heaven. Blessed are you when they despise and persecute you and say all kinds of evil against you falsely for My sake. Rejoice and be very glad, for vast *is* your reward in heaven, for so they persecuted the prophets who were before you."

The disciples looked at each other, not really sure how to wrap their minds around the *persecuted* part of the blessings. Peter was about to question Yeshua but had a better idea. He elbowed Bartholomew in the ribs and prompted the quiet Disciple, who was never one for speaking out loud, to ask Yeshua the question.

"Yeshua?" Bartholomew seemed shocked at the sound of his own voice coming out. "Yeshua... Persecuted? Are we to be despised and spoke of falsely too? When?"

"Bartholomew, anyone who follows me will be persecuted, because I preach a Gospel of Truth to a world that lives in darkness. Do not fear, for the Lord will give you strength in those times, but you have to be light and salt to the world. You must be strong. This is why I have chosen you."

Bartholomew *and* Peter seemed content with Yeshua's answer, so He went on.

"You are the salt of the earth; but if the salt loses its flavor, how will the earth then, be seasoned? It is then good for nothing and can only be thrown out and trampled under the feet of men. You are the light of the world... Think of it this way, a city that is located on a hill cannot be hidden because of the light. Those who live there would not light a lamp and put it under a basket, but on a lamp stand and it gives light to all *who are* in the house. Let your light so shine before men, so that they can see your good works and glorify your Father in heaven."

There seemed to be a change taking place in the Disciples. It was subtle, but I saw it on their faces. Yeshua went on to explain more about The Law, and the sin of the heart.

"Do not think that I came to destroy the Law or the Prophets. I did not come to destroy but to fulfill! Surely... I say to you, until heaven and earth pass away, not one speck or one mark will pass from the Law until all is fulfilled. If anyone breaks one of the least of these commandments, and teaches men to do the same, will be called least in the kingdom of heaven; but whoever does these commandments and teaches them to others, he will be called great in the kingdom of heaven. For I say to you, that unless your righteousness exceeds the righteousness of the scribes and Pharisees, you will by no means enter the kingdom of heaven.

You have heard that it was said to those before you, '*You shall not murder*, and if anyone does commit murder will be in danger of the judgment.' But I say to you that if anyone is angry with his brother without a cause will be in danger of the judgment.' And if anyone says to his brother, 'Raca!' shall be in danger of the council. But if anyone says, 'You fool!' shall be in danger of hell fire."

My recent thought of wanting to kill Judas came to mind. I felt as if he was speaking *directly* to me again.

After talking with the disciples and all of us followers, Yeshua turned His attention to the multitude that was pressing in without relenting. Many were screaming at the top of their lungs for Yeshua to touch them. There were healings of countless people and demons cast out, one right after another. We were all exhausted from trying to keep the crowd from trampling each other and us.

When the crowd dwindled and the sun was close to setting, it finally died down. Yeshua looked more fatigued, by far, than the rest of us. Soon Yeshua was off to pray again while many of us tried to eat something without falling asleep first.

Chapter 23: A Mother's Son

His skin was now cool to the touch. Just after midnight, his skin had still retained a warmth left over from the high fever that took him yesterday evening. Judith continued to wash her son's body with smooth, careful strokes. When he was a baby, she would sing him a lullaby while she bathed him. She did that now, although her smile was one of memory and her song was one of sorrow. The corners of her mouth quivered as she held back a river of tears that would burst forth if she permitted it. One solitary tear ran down her cheek. That's all she would allow for now.

Aryeh was an amazing gift to her and now he was gone. A widowed woman of nearly three years… now had nothing. No husband. No son. No more family. She was now alone.

As she moved the sponge from his forehead down the bridge of his nose, she half expected him to wake up. He seemed so peaceful; as if he were just sleeping. *Wake up Aryeh* she prayed. *Please… wake up*. Her thoughts were interrupted by her best friend coming in the room.

"Judith, I have the linen and spices." She set the materials on the table and softly laid her hand on Judith's shoulder.

"Thank you, Miriam. You have been such a good strength for me through this…" Her words were cut short by the noose that seemed to be around her neck. Miriam put her arm around her and gently squeezed.

"I am here for whatever you need Judith."

I need my son back; can you help me with that?

Judith shook off that spiteful thought toward her friend and responded in kind.

"Thank you, Miriam. I know."

Judith and Miriam carefully wrapped the young man's body in the way according to Jewish custom and called the men in to get the body and begin the journey to the grave site. Aryeh was lifted and placed into to the coffin that would transport him to the tomb. It was at this point that Judith could hold back no longer. The site of her beloved son, finally prepared for burial, set off the grief that had been dammed up for hours. She collapsed into a heap on the floor and wailed with a long, drawn out cry that set anguish into the hearts of all near enough to hear it. Outside the home, the whole city of Nain seemed to turn out for the funeral dirge. Aryeh was well known and liked throughout the small community.

The mother, her friend, and other crying women preceded Aryeh through the streets. Miriam noticed that a small group of men, followed by a large crowd, were directly in their path; unfortunately blocking the way. As the funeral party approached, the group parted to allow the dirge through. Judith was drawn to a certain man with kind eyes. He seemed so concerned. His face was drawn with compassion as they started to pass by.

As Judith neared Yeshua, He spoke to her.

"Do not weep"

The grief struck mother stepped up to Him with questioning eyes as if to say *why are you doing this?* Yeshua reached out and touched the coffin. as he kept his hand there and seemed unwilling to let go, the men carrying Aryeh stopped and stood still. Yeshua looked into the casket.

"Young man, I say to you arise."

Those standing around within earshot of Yeshua looked at Him aghast. Who could be so cold as to speak this way in front of a grieving mother? There was movement in the coffin.

People started screaming as they saw Aryeh sit up and struggle to get out of the linens. The men dropped the coffin in response to the unexpected resurrection and caused Aryeh to expel a loud *huff* as it jarred his body!

Yeshua stepped forward and helped the young man climb out of the casket. Aryeh had managed to loosen his grave clothes and stood there with a bewildered look on his face.

"Mother?"

Yeshua took hold of Judith's hand and presented the son to his mother. Her eyes were wide with excitement, yet unable to comprehend the miracle. Her gaze soon turned from wonderment, to an inescapable sense of relief and awe at having her son standing before her. Judith grabbed her son and held on to him for dear life. In spite of the death grip, Aryeh was able to question her again.

"Mother... what happened? Why am I here wrapped up like this?"

"Aryeh! You were dead! We were on our way to bury you! God has answered my prayer! God has visited us!"

She then proclaimed to everyone around her

"A great prophet has risen up among us!"

Judith turned to thank the prophet who did such a miracle, only to realize, he was now gone. She spun around in a circle, frantically searching the crowd for the man, but to no avail; so she turned her attention back to her living son and blessed God with many tears of joy.

Chapter 24: Love, Prestige and Sacrifice

Aw Capernaum… I loved Capernaum. It now had become my home away from home; kind of like a third cousin, twice removed on my mother's uncle's side. Even now, it was hard to wrap my brain around which time zone I lived in. I was very much acclimated to this world, yet the thought of when I would return to the *other* world, was always hanging on like a bad case of jetlag. I wanted to stay here.

Once again, we stayed at Peter's home, and once again I was reacquainted with Hanna. We seemed to pick up where we left off; however, I was a little more reserved in my feelings toward her this time. There was an ever-increasing dread that this was all too soon coming to an end, and I did not want to encourage something that could not be. Hanna could not disguise her feelings for me. She was young, attractive, and very much ready to be married again.

"Can I fix you something to eat Benjamin?"

"Yes… I would love something to eat."

Hanna lit up at my response and continued kneading a morsel of bread for me. I sat at the table and watched her as she worked. Every so often, I would catch her glancing over at me and giving me a cute little smile. This is difficult. *Why Lord?*

I dismissed my question as foolish and looked around the house for who it was intended. I would have to corner Yeshua again and ask Him how long I will be here. The answer would probably be vague, just as before. Andrew stepped into the room and made his presence known.

"Hanna! I didn't realize you were making something for me to eat. How thoughtful!"

"This is *NOT* for you Andrew!"

A sly expression was revealed on his face as he winked at me and gave *the nod* toward Hanna and smiled at me.

"She will make someone a good wife, eh Benjamin?"

Hanna turned toward her cousin and playfully punched him in the arm.

"Stop it Andrew! Leave Benjamin alone! He can make up his own mind about who he will marry and who he will not!"

Hanna turned her attention to me with a laugh that quickly dissipated. It was obvious by the downcast look on her face that she recognized the gravity in mine. She knew, at that moment that a marriage between us would never be. She dropped what she was doing and put her hands to her mouth and ran out of the room.

"What did I say?" Andrew was puzzled.

"Not to worry my friend. It was nothing *you* said.

I got up and followed after her into the courtyard. She was sitting on an old stone bench looking out toward the countryside. I walked around and knelt in front of her. She kept staring straight ahead as if I weren't there.

"You could have told me."

Tears were gently cascading down her face, matting that cute little curl of hair to her cheek. There was no sobbing or crying out. There was just shallow breathing and a burst of red highlighting her high cheekbones.

"You could have told me you had no intention of marrying me. How could you? How could you speak to me as you have? Have I not given you every corner of my heart? Have you not taken it?"

More tears were flowing now. Hanna then hid her face in her hands and started sobbing. I sat down next to her and tried to contain my own sadness and find the words to say to her.

"Hanna… I am sorry. I had no intention of hurting you. I care for you greatly, and if things were different, I *would* consider you for a wife, but that is not possible. In the beginning, I think I very much wanted this, but my time with Yeshua has changed things."

Was I lying? Was I making this up so I could get out of this predicament? No.

I have a purpose to fulfill, and that means I must follow Yeshua. I cannot marry you and then be gone all the time ministering with Yeshua. You deserve to have someone who can devote their life to you; someone who can stay home with you and raise children. Do you not see how hard this is on Peter's wife and children?"

Hanna looked up with pleading eyes.

"I want to follow Yeshua too! We could do it together! Then, after a while, we could come back here again and have children."

What had I gotten myself into? I *really* cared for Hanna. The last thing I wanted to do was hurt her.

"I'm really sorry Hanna. Forgive me, but I cannot get married."

With that last statement, I got up and walked away while hearing the tender cries of a wonderful woman's heartbreak.

Where was Yeshua? I really needed Him right now. I found Peter visiting with his wife and playing with his children. He looked up at me and smiled.

"Do you know where Yeshua is?" I asked.

"Yes, He is upstairs praying. He spends many hours in prayer these days. Did you see the crowd outside yet?"

"I heard them. It has been growing all morning. Does He plan on ministering soon? If we wait much longer, they will burst in the door!"

Just as I finished speaking, Yeshua stepped off the stairs leading to the roof. He looked around the room as if taking inventory on all of us.

"We must go."

There was a brisk, hard knock at the door. Peter got up and made his way to the door and opened it to find a local Pharisee standing there. Peter threw his head back and rolled his eyes. Simon had been a local Pharisee for many years in Capernaum, and Peter had had a few run-ins with the man and did not care for him.

"What do you want Simon?"

Yeshua immediately broke into the conversation and answered Peter's question.

"Simon is here to invite us to dine with him this day at his house."

Peter tried not to show his disdain for the individual. He knew this man. He had grown up with this man and had never liked him. He was a selfish, self-centered greedy individual; even as a child.

Simon stood there looking perplexed. He hadn't expected Yeshua to know what his intentions were, and yet, that was exactly what his *own* intentions were; to find out if Yeshua really was a prophet or not. He recovered and postured himself in the manner in which a Pharisee should. He straightened his back, lifted his chin and with his hands folded; he spoke with an air of authority.

"Well… yes, as a matter of fact, that is why I *am* here. I would like to extend an invitation to You and your disciples to a feast in *your* honor."

It was obvious that there was no *honor*, whatsoever, intended toward Yeshua. This was all just a ploy to ensnare Him; as was the practice of most Pharisees of late. Yeshua accepted the invitation, to most everyone's dismay, and we all followed Simon to his home.

Where is it?

Items started flying everywhere behind the flailing of hands, sifting through an assortment of accumulation. Kithara had hidden the item here more than a year ago.

Was it stolen? Please…No! It has to be here!

As the mound of worthless items stacked up behind her, her precious treasure finally revealed itself in a shadow of dust and neglect. She grabbed the flask and pulled it free of the nightmare that it represented. This flask of precious spikenard oil was costly… in more ways than one. A stabbing, painful memory shot through heart as she held the cold, tomb-like container. She might as well have held the blood of her only daughter inside of it.

As her mind began to play back the drug induced memory, she reasoned that her daughter would have been better off dead, and her blood kept as a token, than to have ended up where she most likely was now; in the hands of some deranged man groping at her young body.

How could she? How could she sell the one thing, in all of her life that was worth more than any container of oil, gold, or precious stones? It was her only child. They were both starving at the time, and Kithara was under the influence most days and nights, with a revolving door of men in their tiny home.

On one particular evening she was entertaining a slave trader that took an interest in her sleeping daughter. Her judgment was clouded because of a new drug he had convinced her to try. It was like nothing she had ever experienced before, and it left her with no sense of moral, ethical, or motherly instinct. However, when it came to price, she kept the bidding going until it reached a year's wages in precious oil.

She vaguely remembered the cry of her daughter as she was carried away forever. The severity of the situation did not lend itself to reason until the drug had worn off two days later. It was then that her heart was truly broke and it sent her into the deepest depression she had ever known. Being a prostitute, and all the stigmas that came with it, she was able to accept. Selling her own daughter was more than she could bear. She contemplated suicide many times but could never bring herself to do it.

Perhaps today would be different. She thought. Perhaps this man Yeshua could change all of that.

A few hours earlier, as she stood outside watching people pushing through the streets, she noticed some excitement that was taking place close by. She wandered over in that direction and caught hold of the enthusiasm ebbing from the crowd. One man was speaking out about the healing that had taken place in his friend.

"I saw it! I saw it with my own eyes!"

His excitement was egged on by the small circle of people that surrounded his soapbox. His eyes were wide, and his hands were animated as he went on.

"He grew a new arm!"

The crowd gasped in amazement while one man expressed his disbelief.

"You have lost your mind to a demon! No mans arm, which has been missing since birth, can simply grow out a new one!"

Another man spoke up to affirm the tale.

"No... It's true! I saw it as well, along with many other miracles! This Yeshua could be Elijah, returned to us! Not only are His miracles plentiful, but His words as well. He speaks with much wisdom and authority... He even forgives sins!"

"BLASPHEMY!" The skeptic cried. "He is a devil! No one forgives sins but GOD!"

Next to the crowd was a silent minority that waited for the right opportunity to speak. The tale of miracles continued.

"You say this is blasphemy? Do you not know Malchus, who was once paralyzed? He walks now and talks of his healing most often. But it is the healing of the heart that he is most convinced of. You know him... he was a builder who left many in ruin because of his deceitfulness. He has now been rebuilding all that was done wrongly to those people. He lives as a new man, forgiven of his past sins. He is changed. You cannot deny that! Can this wonderful thing come from Satan? I say no!"

Now was the right opportunity for those standing in the shadows to speak.

"We shall see if this man is Elijah, or a prophet come from God. Even now, Simon the Pharisee has asked Yeshua to his home. He means to find out who this man really is. They are going there now.

Kithara now had confirmation. She had heard of this Yeshua but was not fully convinced that He could help her. She had both of her arms and legs. The only thing she needed was a new heart... just like this man called Malchus. She would seek Him out and give Him her most valuable possession in exchange for a new heart... if it were possible.

The Pharisee's house was in an area Kithara did not frequent very often, unless she was summoned there in the wee hours of the night. Now, during the daylight hours, people who walked by were looking at her with disgust on their faces. She was out of her element here and feeling very vulnerable.

As she neared Simon's dwelling, she noticed a crowd was already starting to gather outside. No attention was drawn toward the house, so she guessed that they had not yet arrived. How was she going to see Yeshua? How would she get inside? She tucked her valuable cache of oil close to her body so as not to be dropped or easily stolen from her. The butterflies in her stomach were working overtime as she stared down the street in desperation.

Please come quickly Yeshua!

Suddenly, a commotion was heard and the throng of people surrounding Simon's house perked up; straining their necks to see Yeshua coming.

There He was… out in front of the group. She clutched the alabaster flask so tight; she thought she would shatter it. She slighted her grip and began searching for a way to get to Him. There was a cloak, draped over the side of a cart; she grabbed it and covered herself. She was bumped then by a few servant girls pushing their way past her. She quickly picked up their cadence, blended in, and walked inside with them. Once indoors, she slipped into the shadows; trying to go unnoticed until the right time.

Yeshua entered the house along with His Disciples, and many others who came along, or were invited for the dinner. Next came Simon. He paused at the door where one servant removed his shoes and proceeded to wash his feet while the other held a basin in front of him so he could wash his hands. He then took his place at the head of the table.

Yeshua was at the table facing away from Kithara.

Now that I am here, how to I approach such a Holy Man? She thought.

Will He take this gift? Will He reject me?

She did the first thing that came to her mind. Out of desperation, she ran forward and fell at Yeshua' feet and started crying. Tears started to pour out of her eyes as she contemplated the unworthiness of her plea. She did not deserve forgiveness for what she had done. Her whole life was a wreck of bad decisions and a constancy of sin.

If forgiveness was given or not, she had to try, or she could no longer live with herself.

Yeshua had removed His shoes, and His feet were laid bare right in front of her. The anguish inside of her began to explode as she bent forward and kissed the soles of His feet; the lowest part of His body. Her tears washed away the dust that covered them, and she started wiping them down with her hair. This Man did not strike her down. He did not verbally condemn her. He continued to allow her to humble herself before Him in the presence of so many people who despised her. This made her weep all the more. Kissing His feet and washing them with her tears. She felt the eyes of the dinner party burning into her, but she didn't care. Nothing would interfere with honoring this Man.

Next, she took the fragrant oil and poured it on His feet. The smell permeated the home and enraged the hearts of some of those present. Simon was livid!

How could this Man be a prophet? Does he not know what this woman is? How could He let her touch Him? She is a sinner! She is unclean! He is no prophet!

Other minds were condemning her too, not just Simon. Then Yeshua turned toward the woman and smiled. He gently placed His hand on top of her head and proceeded to ask Simon a question.

"Simon, I have something to tell you."

"Yes, please say it Teacher"

"There was a certain man who had two debtors. One owed five hundred denarii, and the other fifty. And when they had no way of repaying, he freely forgave them both of their debt. Tell Me Simon, which of these men will love him more for what he had done?

"I suppose the one whom he forgave more."

"You are right. Now, do you see this woman? I came into your home and you gave Me no water to wash My feet, yet she has washed My feet with her tears and wiped them with her own hair. You gave Me no kiss as a customary greeting, yet this woman has not stopped kissing My feet since I sat down here! You did not anoint My head with oil, yet she has sacrificed much to anoint My feet with her fragrant oil. Listen carefully to Me. Her sins, which are many, are now forgiven. She has loved much. But to whom little is forgiven, the same loves little."

Yeshua turned his attention back to Kithara and said

"Your sins are forgiven."

Immediately, those who were at the table began to grumble and think to themselves *who is this that He can forgive sin?*

"Woman, your great faith has saved you. Go now in peace."

Chapter 25: Peace Be Still

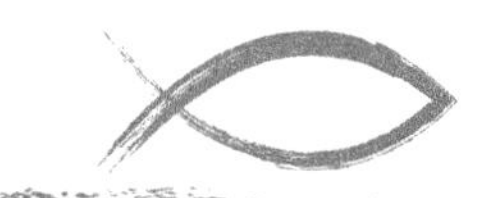

My heart was heavy… in the midst of so many miracles, and so much teaching by Yeshua, I was still troubled in my heart. Had I accepted Yeshua as my *Lord and Savior*, as they say? Yes. Had my life been changed forever? Yes. I wanted to serve Him with all that was in me. Then what was this conflict in my heart?

I had to leave the group to find a secluded spot to pray. I found one next to a tiny brook. The current was just strong enough to provide an audible *bubbling* and an oasis of solitude. I sat down on the small bank and tried to find the words to pray. If Yeshua had shown an example of anything lately, it was definitely prayer. He went *often* to The Father in prayer; sometimes taking the place of precious sleep. I was worn out, and He just kept on going. A lesson to be learned, I suppose. I broke into a fervent, honest prayer.

Father God. . . How can I be so troubled? Please help me to know Your will. Continue to show me the right way to live out my life through Your Son, Yeshua. I have been so consumed with selfishness. What I want. . . What I need. Even in the areas of how I should serve You! I want to stay here. I don't want to go back to my old life. The world is a mess, and people are even more hardened in their hearts toward You than they are here. Father, regardless of my feelings, I want YOU to have your will in my life.

I poured out my soul for at least an hour and then made my way back to camp. When I got there, Nathaniel was waiting for me.

"My brother, we must go. The others have already set out for Nazareth on foot. Where have you been?"

"I am sorry Nathaniel; I was off praying."

"Ah, prayer is a good reason for being late. Come, we will catch up with the others. Yeshua and the Disciples have gone across the Lake. We were told to wait for them In Nazareth."

Peter loved sailing, because his life had always been on the water. From the time he was old enough to walk, his father had taught him to sail and to fish. These were some of his fondest memories and it was *these* memories that now haunted him. The Sea of Galilee could give life in the abundance of fish that it provided, yet with its volatile North Winds, it could also take life. This time of year, winds would often sweep down through the gorges from Mt Herman, suddenly causing great storms on the lake that have taken many lives. His father had disappeared in a storm like that and was presumed drowned. It was a bitter-sweet moment as Peter felt the wind pick up.

Waves began to rock the boat quite heavily and the sail was full of its force. They could make good time across the lake if it stayed at present strength, but Peter knew better. This was the beginning of a good-sized thunderstorm. Matthew was holding on to the side of the boat with white-knuckle panic and a face that was set in terrifying determination. He had never sailed before. He was a city dweller with absolutely no experience on the sea whatsoever. Suddenly, large drops of rain began to fall. It pelted their faces and immediately drenched their garments.

"Lower the sail and go to oars!"

Peter screamed over the tumult and fought against the powerful jerks of the rudder he was manning. Andrew took charge of the crew and had them fix the oars and go to work. Waves began cascading over the sides of the boat now, and they were taking on water… fast! The situation was rather desperate, and everyone knew it. As James strained his muscles against the pull of the oars, he finally noticed Yeshua was still lying at the front of the boat. Waves and rain were hitting Him full on and He was not moving. James feared he was dead.

"Yeshua!" James yelled.

No response.

"John! Is Yeshua drowned? Go to Him!"

John frantically made his way toward Yeshua, thrown to one side of the boat and to the other. Finally, he reached Him and shook Him.

"LORD YESHUA! We perish! Save us Yeshua!"

Yeshua woke from His slumber and sat up. His eyes fixed on the men as He braced Himself against the storm's madness. Yeshua yelled above the noise

"Why are you so fearful? Where is your faith?"

Yeshua stood up and spoke in a thundering voice that commanded submission.

"PEACE! BE STILL!"

The wind and the sea responded immediately. The sea subsided its tumult. All that remained above the silence of the wind, was the gentile lapping of the waves against the side of the boat. Each man present was speechless, except for Peter who spoke out in almost a whisper.

"Who can this be, that even the winds and the sea obey Him?"

Mark took a deep breath and slipped his oar back into the water, signaling the rest to get busy and start rowing. Peter continued to stare in wonderment. Miracles of great measure, he has seen. But this miracle was at another level, entirely escaping his means of understanding. He looked around at the rest and saw the same wonderment on their faces... all except Matthew, that is. His hands were still riveted to the side of the boat with a death grip and his eyes were still wide with fear. Suddenly he snapped out of his trance and started a coughing fit. He spit and sputtered, trying to get all the water out of his lungs. Andrew tried to help by slapping him on the back but only succeeded in angering him.

"Leave me be! I will perish before my time! Why, oh why must we sail out into the middle of this forsaken lake to be drowned! I do NOT like sailing! I am made to walk on land, not die at the bottom of the sea!"

Everyone laughed at his comical rant, but Peter calmly spoke to reassure him.

"Matthew... look around you. The storm has ceased."

Matthew closed his eyes tight then reopened them, as if to clear out the panic bouncing around in his head. He took a steady look around and finally noticed that they were out of harm's way. A look of relief softened the fear that was etched on his face.

"We... what... what happened? How can this be?"

Yeshua put His hand on Matthew's shoulder and answered his question.

"Matthew, you *must* learn to have faith."

The poor, wet soul, lowered his head to his chest and began to cry softly; expressing what every other man on the boat wished they could do, but didn't. The rest of the journey was made in reflective silence.

Chapter 26: Barsabas the Demoniac

On the east coast of the Sea of Galilee, the rocky beach turned into an incline that rose up to a jagged outcropping of rocks. In a fissure between the rocks was a deep, dark entrance to a tomb. In times past, truth became tales, and tales became legends as parents shared the horrors of the wild man to their children. So outlandish, or seemingly so, were these stories, that no child would dare go up to the tombs for fear of being eaten by the feral beast.

Many times, the children would play at a distance and see shadows up in the rocks and horrible screams echoing out of the burial places. Then there were times when stones were thrown from unseen hands at them, and large rocks rolling down the mountainside, almost crushing them.

Waves were just crashing on the shoreline minutes ago. But it was quiet now… eerily quiet. The wind stopped as fast as someone blowing out a candle, and the sound of the waves ceased their pounding of the beach. The only thing that could be heard was the faint shuffling of feet on the floor of the cave, and the heavy breathing of a man tormented. In the dim light, drops of blood could be seen dripping and pooling up in the dust on the floor as sharp rocks gouged and cut the skin.

Yes… that feels good. You must feel the pain! Stop the voices in your head!

Two orbs in the twilight of the cave, were narrowed into thin slits as Barsabas grimaced against the pain. He would endure this for as long as it takes. *HE* wanted control, but it was a losing battle. He could feel them rising up against his will again. The cutting would only last for so long. Suddenly, an unearthly scream escaped his lips and his body went into a convulsion. He bounced around on the floor like a fish out water. They were coming.

"You cannot resist us Barsabas! We are many, and we SHALL take you! We OWN you!"

His body straightened out stiff like a board and froze. He seemed helpless in their grip.

"Yes! You are ours to do with as we please!"

"There is nothing you can do! We are too many!"

Many more voices continued to torment his mind and body. He regained his thoughts and motor functions again, briefly, and began cutting.

"Noooooo! Leave me be!"

Barsabas began striking his head with the rock as he ran out of the cave in a blinding rage, screaming…

"I don't want you! Leave me alone!" Barsabas' foot caught the root of a bush and it sent him tumbling down the mountainside, over sharp rocks and thorn bushes. Each impact was a collision of skin, bone, and blood. He could feel his bones breaking with each contact with the rock. When he finally came to a stop, he lay just up from the beach with blood filling his eyes and his mouth.

In spite of the injuries, he felt massive relief. The pain was immense, but with pain came temporary freedom from the demons that taunted him. He wiped the blood from his eyes and noticed some shapes walking up from the beach. He tried to cry out but was struck mute. They were here again, and they racked his body with more force than he could withstand.

His broken bones were no obstacle to the strength of the demons. He rose from his prone position to a standing one. His body was like a rag doll. The demons manipulated it in spite of his inability to physically walk. He started sprinting toward the figures at a dead run.

Luke was the first to notice the strange, naked form approaching them. It was a mangled, dirty, bloody mess of what he gathered to be a human being. His eyes were most noticeable. They were almost solid white from them being rolled back in his head. His teeth were bared and gnashing out like a dog as he ran. Luke's first instinct was to run, but then Yeshua stopped and waited. The wild man came up short of Yeshua and threw himself on the ground at His feet. The voice coming out of him was horrific and mingled, like more than one voice. It sent the hair rising up on the back of his neck.

"What have I to do with You, Yeshua, Son of the Most High God? I implore You by God that you do not torment me!"

"Come out of the man, unclean spirit!"

The man's body twisted and contorted and then bowed before Yeshua.

"What is your name?"

"My name is Legion; for we are many! Please, I beg of you, do not send us out of the country!"

There was the sound of pigs nearby, on the side of the mountain. The herd was being grazed on top of a small shelf of land jetting out into the sea. The demon set its gaze on the pigs and pleaded again with Yeshua.

"Send us into the swine, that we may enter them!"

Yeshua pointed in the direction of the herd and said "Go!"

Immediately, the spirits came out of the man and entered the large herd of pigs. It was as if someone shot a gun in the air. The herd of swine jumped into motion, trampling each other and everything in their path as they pushed toward the cliff. The herders were screaming at the top of their lungs, trying to contain the beasts, but to no avail. A line of pigs, at least fifty or more wide, one line after another poured over the precipice like a waterfall. They crashed into the sea and drowned – every one of them. The men who herded the swine fled the scene in fear, for none had experienced anything like this before, and now *they* would be held responsible for the tragedy. The owners of the herd would be out about two thousand pigs. They ran toward the city of Decapolis and told all what had happened.

Barsabas sat on the rocky beach with his head in his hands. Different places on his body were bruised and bulging out where bones were obviously broken and almost breaking through the skin. He was shaking uncontrollably.

Yeshua motioned for John to get a cloak to cover Barsabas with, then stepped forward and placed his hand on him. Instantaneously, the shaking stopped; the swelling and bruising disappeared… and the years of abuse and neglect of his body were no longer visible. John got back with the cloak and covered him, then offered him a hand up.

"What is your name?"

"Barsabas" he quietly whispered as the realization came across his face. "I… I am free!" His eyes were bright and his smile broad as he started jumping up and down. "I am free! They are gone! The spirits are gone!"

His party was soon interrupted by some very irate men. They yelled at Yeshua.

"You! You there! What have you done to my herd?"

His attention drifted toward the man in the cloak. His eyes flashed with the recognition of this man. This was the demon possessed man from the tombs. *How can this be? This man is sane, and clean!*

"This is the work of something I have never seen before. This man is now whole?" He looked around at the crowd of people gathered there. "How did this happen?"

He gathered bits and pieces of the story as best he could as the witnesses talked over each other in their excitement. He stepped back in a panic and shouted again at Yeshua.

"Please… You must leave us! Depart our land!"

Yeshua and the Disciples turned toward the boat to leave.

"No… wait My Lord! Please, take me with you! I want to serve you, for you have saved me from a life of terrible bondage!"

"No Barsabas, you must stay. Go home to your friends and tell them what great things the Lord has done for you, and how He has had compassion on you."

Barsabas hung his head and contemplated the idea of seeing his old friends… friends who had all but given up hope in ever seeing him again. It was bittersweet to him. He wanted so, to follow this wonderful Man who had saved him. Yet, he longed to have his normal life back. For too many years, his mind had been ravaged with demons, and now the Man who changed his life is telling him to go back home. He would, and he would tell *everyone* about this wonderful Man of God.

"Master, I will do as You say, and I will proclaim what You have done to all the city of Decapolis!"

Yeshua smiled as Barsabas embraced Him. The former demonic turned and ran, rejoicing as he made his way for home. Yeshua and the disciples returned to the boat and made their way south, back to Tiberius… and then Nazareth.

Chapter 27: The Hem of His Garment

In a secluded area on the outskirts of Nazareth, a small dwelling lay dark and void of many furnishings. There was only the least of necessities. Every means of wealth available had been traded for the assistance of doctors and healers. All that was left was a bed, and one chair for a caring mother to sit on as she fretted over her dying child.

"How are you feeling this morning Phebe?"

Phebe tried to answer but was too weak to respond just now. Most days she was bed ridden… today was no different. She slowly sat up in bed and reached for a cup of water by her bedside. The water soothed her vocal cords enough to talk.

"I will be fine, mother. I just need a little time to get moving this morning."

"I have already changed your garments. I did it while you were sleeping. They should last through the morning."

Phebe was heartbroken. Her mother has had to care for her for far too long now. She has faced too many difficulties for a woman her age while having to care for an invalid daughter. For the first two years of her condition, her husband took care of her. But when the money was all given to physicians with no change in her health, he left one morning without a word. From that point on, it was just her and her mother.

"Mother, why do you continue to care for me? I can manage by myself. You don't have to keep doing this."

Phebe's mother gave her a stern look and rebuked her daughter.

"You *will* not tell me when I can or cannot care for you! Phebe, you are my daughter. Asking me to leave you alone to care for yourself, would cause me to die an early death! Do you want that?" Her firm look softened, and tears could be seen pooling up in her eyes. Phebe realized how fortunate she was to have her mother.

"I'm sorry mother. I *do* appreciate all that you do for me, and I *could* not make it on my own. But, how much longer can we go on like this? I grow weaker every day and we are out of money."

"Yes, I know Phebe, but I have heard rumors. I was told that the man named Yeshua is here. He has been in the city teaching and many have been healed. I only pray that He can help you. I do not know where he is now, but I am going to go and find Him, now that you are awake."

"Do you really think this Yeshua can heal me? I have seen so many promises given to me, only to fail. I cannot live with another disappointment."

"Trust in God Daughter. This Man of God is sure to deliver you. He has done so much, there is no doubt that He is a Prophet. Lay still now. I am going to look for Him and will return shortly."

Phebe's mother placed her hand on her precious daughter's forehead and quietly prayed that she would live until she brought back the Man of God. It was evident that time was short. She then turned and left the dwelling in search of hope.

Yeshua was never at a loss for words, and never at a loss of strength. The schedule we kept would put most traveling Evangelists to shame. Simon and I were constantly tired and found ourselves often wondering if it was all worth it. It's funny how even in the presence of Yeshua, the flesh was still weak. But on those occasions where we saw lives changed, healed, and delivered... we would be encouraged to keep on keeping on.

Once again, in the City of Nazareth, the mood had changed somewhat. People were more receptive to Yeshua and were flocking to see Him. It was difficult to keep people from trampling Him, *and* us, for that matter! As we made our way toward the center of the city, the streets narrowed, and the congestion grew. Nathaniel called out to Yeshua and yelled above the crowd

"Yeshua! We have to find a way out of here! People are fighting each other to get close to You!"

"Nathaniel... we are almost where we need to be. Do not fear."

Phebe had been awakened by a sudden bang on the door. As her mind cleared, she realized that there was a loud commotion in the street outside. She could see the heads of people slowly moving by her window. Her door rattled from the constant pressure of bodies being pushed against it as the throng fought to move forward. As she pondered what was causing such a commotion, she heard someone yelling above the noise of the crowd. It was right outside her door. She heard the name *Yeshua* being called out. *Could it be HIM? Could it be the very man that her mother set out to find?*

With all of her strength, all of her will, and a last desperate attempt to change her demise... Phebe forced her body into submission and fought her way out of bed. Her head reeled, causing the room to spin in circles. As she limbered toward the door, her body quaked uncontrollably because of the strain suddenly thrown upon it. She paused and caught her breath as she reached the door. Leaning up against it, her body seemed to amplify every vibration as the people outside continued to bump up against it. As she stood there… she felt the blood flowing out of her at a faster rate now. Being on her feet always sped up the flow of blood. She could actually feel her life slipping away. *I have to get to Him… This is it; I HAVE to!*

Phebe grabbed hold of the latch, took a deep breath, and opened the door. She was almost thrown backward as some people spilled into her little house. They looked surprised and taken back. One was a woman, and she recognized right away what the situation was.

"She is unclean!" She pointed at her with condemnation, but Phebe was un-phased by it. She had her eyes set on Yeshua now, and there was nothing that could keep her from Him! As people began to hear and respond to the declaration of *uncleanness*, some of the crowd began to step back from her, while others were still oblivious to the situation. Although the crowd ahead of her lessened, she still had to push her way ahead. *If I could just touch His clothes, I would be healed!*

Her strength was about to let out, and her body was being battered by the crowd as she pressed on. Just as she was reaching for Yeshua, she was tripped and went headlong into the sea of people around her. She landed with a bone crushing jar and thought it could be over, but she would not stop now! She edged up on to her elbows and then lunged forward the few feet between her and Yeshua. As she stretched her hand out in one last ditch effort, her weak, frail hand grasped the back of Yeshua' garment. Immediately, everything slowed down to a frame by frame, movie like moment, in High Definition detail. Every speck of dust lingering in the air was hung in suspension. The feet surrounding her were stopped in mid stride and each leather sandal showed distinctive cracks with years of wear on them. Every pore in the skin of her hand could be seen and every strand of fiber in Yeshua' garment showed the exquisite craftsmanship of an expert weaver. As soon as her grip secured itself in the folds of Yeshua' clothing, a powerful wave of energy seemed to expel itself from the Son of God! Her body absorbed most of it, but some of it shot through the crowd and caused everyone to stop and wonder what had just happened. Yeshua immediately called out to His disciples.

"Who touched me?" Those who were walking with Him looked at each other in amazement. Peter answered.

"Master, the people are pressing in from every side, and You say, 'Who touched me?'

"Somebody touched Me. For I perceived power going out from Me."

Phebe rose from the ground trembling; and humbly faced Yeshua.

"Lord, it was I who touched You! For I knew that if I but touch, even the hem of your garment, I would be healed... and it is so!" Yeshua looked with compassion on her.

"Daughter... be of good cheer; your faith has made you well. Go in peace."

Phebe wiped the tears from her eyes, turned, and walked back toward her home. It had been a long time since she felt any energy. Right now, she felt as if she could run and never stop. As she lifted her gaze, she locked eyes her mother standing in the distance. She had her hands over her mouth and tears were streaming down her face. Her daughter was healed! Her daughter was whole once again!

I stood there for just a moment longer as mother and daughter locked in an embrace. I miss my daughter...

Chapter 28: Herod's Birthday Party

King Herod was known to be extravagant with his parties, but this one was spectacular! It was *his* birthday and he pulled out all the stops! Herodias was equal to the task.

"Salome, my dearest daughter, let me speak with you privately." Herodias pulled her beautiful daughter into an adjoining room in order to share her plot. "I want you to dance for your uncle."

"What? Mother, no! Please… I am not going to dance for that man! He is *your* pleasure, not mine. Why don't *you* dance for him?"

"Because, this is a special day," she paused with an irritated stare, "and he and his guests are deserving of a more, shall we say, *younger* form of entertainment. I want you to dance in a way that captures his heart. If you do this right, he will grant you any wish you desire."

"But I *have* no wish for anything!" Salome turned away from her mother to leave but was yanked back by her arm.

"You *WILL* dance for him, and you *WILL* do it as I say! I have need of something and you will help me get it!"

A single drip of water echoed in his cell with a steady rhythm and reliable cadence.

Down here, there was no sound of the outside world, only the drip of water and the scurrying of rats looking for his morsel of stale bread. At least the rats were enjoying it. John prayed silently. Fettered to the wall, he gave thanks for God's love and for the coming of His Son. John felt humbled by the awesome opportunity he had had to prepare the way for Yeshua. There were no feelings of remorse in this cold wet cell; no anger toward a God that would allow him to be imprisoned. His heart was fulfilled, and there was nothing that could take that away from him. John raised his hands, pulling the links of chains through the rings attached to the stone floor. The sound bounced off the walls in a metallic cadence, matching the rhythm of his words. He worshipped God.

Herod gazed out over his throng of guests. All of the important men were here. High- ranking soldiers, Politicians, and Nobles. Every one of them speak in such great admiration of him in his presence, but he knew that their hearts were far from praise and adoration. They would speak of him in spiteful ways behind his back. He had heard them do so when they were unaware of his presence from behind a wall or around a corner. Herod's heart sank and his mind struggled with the words of John. John spoke that love, peace and forgiveness could be found in Yeshua The Messiah. *Peace... what is peace* he thought. He has *longed* for it many times but has never known it. *Love*? He thought that he loved Herodias, but even *she* didn't satisfy this emptiness in his heart. He longed for true love. As if on cue, Salome moved into his line of vision. Before, it was blurred by his thoughts. Now... he was focused. She was *soooo* beautiful! A crooked smile formed on his lips as the musicians started. First the drumbeat. Her body started moving with the beat and her hands gracefully gathered the stares of all who were present. She had to admit it... she *liked* the attention! Then the music began. Each note was defined and intentional; each instrument in sync with her dancing. The more they stared with longing in their eyes, the more intense her dance would become. The music increased in volume and her eyes flashed... yearning for Herod's attention. She held his gaze and saw him slide to the edge of his throne... leaning forward... drinking in her *intoxicating* dance. He was so captured by her beauty; he *would* give her anything. She worked her way through the crowd ignoring their cheers and reaching hands. Her focus stayed the course. She must win Herod's desire. The music slowed to a crawl, like a heart giving up its life; each beat slower than the one before. She moved up each step toward Herod... closer and closer. He was hers. She completed her dance by sitting on his lap and draping her arms around his neck. She leaned in and spoke ever so softly to him.

"Hello Uncle. Did you enjoy my dancing?" His mind was labored, and his eyes were fixed on hers.

"Ask whatever you want of me and I will give you up to half of my kingdom." There it was. She had accomplished just what her mother said she would. Now she had the authority to ask him for anything.

"Bring me..." Herod leaned in closer to her.

"Yes, my love? Anything... please, ask." Salome quickly stood up and walked down the steps to her waiting mother.

"What should I ask of him, mother?" She turned around and faced Herod with a mischievous smile on her face. Herod's countenance fell as he realized his authority had been compromised. Without needing to, her mother whispered in her ear then stepped back with a look of contempt on her face that said everything. Salome shouted loud enough for everyone to hear.

"I want John the Baptist's head on a platter! Bring it to me HERE! She stomped her foot and pointed to the floor in front of her.

Near Bethsaida, Yeshua had been ministering all day as usual and we followers were taking in as much as we could with the rest of the crowd. Yeshua, the week prior, had sent out the disciples as sort of an initiation. They were to share the Gospel, heal the sick, and cast out demons... without the help of Yeshua. They were on their own. Simon and I wished we could have gone along, but there was plenty to do here with Yeshua. Simon noticed a few men approaching Yeshua.

"Who do you think *that* is my friend?" It was apparent that Yeshua knew who they were by his welcoming smile, but that soon changed. His smile turned to tears as the men shared their hearts with Him. They were crying as they left. We went to Yeshua to find out what was going on. As I walked up to Yeshua, he looked up. I had never seen such sorrow in his eyes before. He spoke to us.

"John, my cousin, is dead." Simon and I looked at each other in shock. "Herod had him executed yesterday. He was beheaded."

Seeing Yeshua like this opened up a whole new aspect of Him that I had never seen. Grief. If Yeshua was God, wouldn't He know that John the Baptist was in Abraham's bosom now? Why would Yeshua grieve over John? This was the part of Yeshua that showed that he was *all* human and *all* God at the same time. In fact, God grieves over the sin in our lives. God grieves over an unrepentant Israel. Why wouldn't He grieve for a wonderful man of God and for his hurting family?

Chapter 29: Five Thousand Miracles

Yeshua needed time away so He went by boat down the shoreline to be alone. Within the hour, we started to see an extreme influx of seekers. There were thousands of people showing up to see and hear Yeshua. It wasn't long before He was found by the multitude and when Yeshua saw it, He had compassion on them and began ministering to them.

The disciples returned just in time. We who had remained were beginning to get overrun by the throng of new people who had shown up. Yeshua had been healing the sick for hours now, and He was still going strong. Peter approached us with a great determination on his face.

"We heard the news of John the Baptist. We came as soon as we could. Yeshua must stop. The hour is getting late. There are too many now and they just keep coming!"

I filled Peter in on the details of the day.

"As soon as Yeshua found out about John, He tried to get away and be alone, but the crowds just kept coming. He came back to shore and started ministering to them about four hours ago. We have had a hard time preventing the people from over running Him."

Peter was concerned and quickly approached Yeshua to provide an *intervention*.

"Rabbi, we are far from a city, and evening will be upon us soon. Send the crowds away so they can go into the villages and buy food for themselves." Yeshua responded in a way that surprised us all.

"No need to send them away. *You* give them food to eat."

"Lord, we have here only five loaves and two fish." Peter was at a loss for words as to what Yeshua had planned here.

"Bring the loaves and fish to me."

Yeshua told the crowd to be seated on the grass and a hush fell over the hungry seekers. That was a miracle in itself. I have never seen such authority in all my life as to where a simple few words could quiet a mob of people!

Yeshua took the loaves and fish and gazed toward the heavens. He blessed and broke the bread, then handed it to the disciples to distribute to the weary people. As each basket was passed between them, the baskets remained full. After an hour or so, the remaining food came back. Twelve baskets... FULL! When God gives... He gives in a big way!

There are many instances in life that need to be treasured. When you see five thousand people fed from a few loaves and fish... when you see people crying after having their sins forgiven... when you see the love in Yeshua's eyes, there is no comparison.

Chapter 30: The Storm

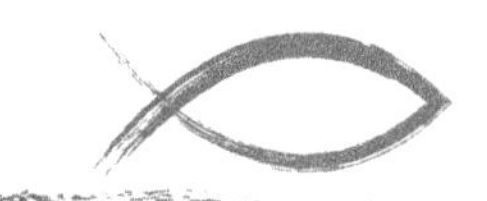

After the miracles and the teaching had come to a close, Yeshua told the disciples to get in a boat and cross over to the land of Gennesaret where he would later meet them. Yeshua stayed to send away the crowds and then find a place to pray.

As Andrew and James helped the others into the boat, Peter stood on the shoreline gazing at the sky. To a normal person, there may have not been any sign of trouble on the horizon; but to a seasoned fisherman, there were all the makings of a storm brewing… here we go *again*!

The Sea of Galilee was nestled in a precarious spot. Being over six hundred feet below sea level with mountains to the East reaching two thousand feet, it was a recipe for rapid change. When the cool air of the mountains would sweep down and meet the moist tropical climate of the sea, dangerous squalls could develop within moments.

Andrew and Peter exchanged a glance of concern. Yeshua would not send them into harm's way, yet experience told them otherwise. None-the-less, they would press on. Peter had more reservations about setting sail than his brothers did. They were too young to remember the death of their father. Peter's mind recalled every moment vividly. It was an evening not unlike this one. He and his mother stood on the shore waiting for his father to return from fishing. He would never return. Peter suffered greatly from guilt, because he was supposed to have gone along with his father that day. A surge of wind brought Peter back to the present, almost losing his footing.

"Peter!" Andrew exclaimed. "Is it wise to sail?"

"Andrew, we must do as Yeshua said."

Peter waded the rest of the way to the boat and attempted to aid the last remaining person left to board. Matthew was taking his own sweet time getting in the boat. Peter grabbed Matthew's arm in an attempt to help him up.

"Let go of me! I'll do this in my own time!"

"We could have been to the other side by now if we didn't have to wait on you Matthew!" James quipped. The others burst out in laughter.

"Keep laughing at my expense!" said Matthew. "YOU may be used to not being on dry land, but I am NOT! In case you don't remember, I nearly drowned the last time we were out on this endless sea of peril! I don't understand why we can't just walk around it like normal people do!" Matthews face was red with anger and his eyes full of fear. It was hard not to feel sorry for the man.

"Have faith my brother." said Peter. "Yeshua saved us from that plight, don't you remember? We will see no harm." Matthew softened a little.

"Well, what are you waiting for.... Help me into this death trap!" Peter obliged and stifled a laugh. Once seated, Matthew gripped the side of the boat with white knuckled terror and sat in a huff.

Mark and Thomas readied the sail. Raising the main halyard, the sail snapped-to and lunged the boat forward with a jerk. Matthew shrieked as he flew backwards, landing on Nathaniel's lap. Matthew quickly recovered himself and muted a few curse words under his breath. Then, he grabbed the nearest rope and fastened it around his torso. He tied himself off to a cleat and set his eyes forward, not saying another word. Peter took control of the rudder, praying under his breath that they weren't headed for trouble.

Smooth sailing, it was not! They were, however, making good time. Up until then, the sea was nothing that Peter couldn't handle, but he could sense the uptick in the rhythm of the sea. They were about to experience some rough weather. Almost on cue, the wind picked up and the rain started to fall. An audible groan escaped the disciples. Peter took charge of the situation.

"Go to oars! Now!"

Mark and James brought down the sail and tied it off, while the rest fought against the turbulence of the boat to ready the oars. Peter was growing tired of fighting the rudder; just like last time, it was all he could do to keep it under control.

Lightening split the night sky and lit up the faces of the crew. Even the ones with experience on the sea seemed frightened. Matthew's eyes were wide with fear as a long and eerie scream escaped lips.

"A spirit! Over there! We are going to perish!"

The sailors turned and fixed their eyes on what Matthew was fearfully shaking his finger at. Their eyes grew wide with fear themselves, as they beheld the specter. It was unaffected by the wind and the waves while moving closer to the disciples. Then a voice was heard above the tumult.

"Don't be afraid! It is I."

Peter recognized that voice. It was Yeshua's.

"Lord, if it is really you... Ask me to come to you on the water!"

"Come!"

Peter straddled the edge of the boat and tried to feel out a firm footing with the tip of his toes. The rising and falling of the boat made it impossible to feel anything but the seas rolling waves. With childlike faith, Peter took in a deep breath and swung his leg over and jumped. His feet met a solid foundation that jarred his knees. He was standing on the sea. His eyes fixed, he started walking towards Yeshua. It was like a dream, yet very real in the physical sense. Without warning, there was a loud CRACK as lightning struck the top of the mast on the fishing boat and set the wood ablaze for a moment. The disciples screamed and Peter turned in fear toward the chaos behind him. It was then that he plunged beneath the waves like a rock. He was surrounded in darkness, except for the occasional green illumination from the lightening above the waves. He fervently kicked his feet in an effort to make his way back to the surface; however, his clothing weighed him down and seemed to make him sink faster the more he struggled. It was quiet and peaceful down there, while the storm raged in all of its fury above. He could give in and just let the sea take him; an easier solution to be sure, but that would have to be another time... he was not ready to give up just yet! He stretched out his hand and prayed for deliverance from his ultimate demise. As if on cue, a hand reached beneath the surface and grabbed hold of Peter's hand, raising him up from the depths of certain death to the comforting arms of Yeshua.

"Peter! Why do you doubt?"

The wind and the waves began to die down. When they reached the boat and climbed in, Peter looked around. The sea was calm, and they were already just offshore at their destination.

Chapter 31: The Bethsaida Blind Man

As they entered Bethsaida, it was obvious that Yeshua was *Rock Star Status*. Everywhere we go now, it's the same. People screaming, chanting, and swarming Him. Simon and I began to get separated. We were buffeted from every side!

"Benjamin! I am losing my patience with these people! Let's press over to the side of that building and get out of this chaos for a moment!"

I followed the back of his head and kept a visual bead on Yeshua and the disciples, as best I could. As I fought my way through, I could feel the electricity in the air! Every soul had the same expression on their face... desperation. Men had thrown their man-cards in the dirt and trampled them underfoot; no regard for pride at all. Most were crying. Some were angry. Many were frustrated for not being able to get close to the Son of God. Close enough for the miracle each man desired. A healing for a loved one, or himself? Forgiveness for adultery, greed, or bad business dealings? A longing for the great chasm of emptiness to be filled somehow? My heart sank. There are so many souls in this World... now, and for many generations to come, that need what only The Father can provide! Instead of providing a path to Yeshua, we spend our lives sucking up social media, sports, and entertainment instead of getting out there and sharing the Kingdom with hurting people!

When I reached Simon, he was helping a man to his feet. He looked to be a beggar. He was, at best guess, middle aged, but worn. Then I noticed his demeanor… he was blind. Simon had this man by the elbow and was proceeding to guide the man to Yeshua, but he resisted. Leaning back against the wall, he tried to slide down to a seated position again. Simon questioned him.

"Do you not wish to be made whole? Don't you wish to see again? You were calling out to Yeshua… I thought you wanted this?"

"I… I did not say I wanted this! Yes, I may have called out His name, but I never thought He would hear me anyway. Besides, I am nothing… Nobody! I don't even deserve it! You don't know my life! I am satisfied right here. This is *MY* place in this town! I do not wish to leave it!"

"You do not understand. We are *with* Yeshua. We travel with Him. We can get you to Him! What is your name?"

The man bit his bottom lip to keep his mouth from quivering. The turmoil of this decision was written all over his face.

"My name is Neriah"

"Come with us Neriah… we will get you to Him!"

The blind man nodded his head in agreement. Simon and I got on both sides of him and led him through the crowd to Yeshua. It took some work, fighting the resistance of the people, and the fact that Neriah was dragging his feet. He was *very* uncomfortable being out of his element. It's obvious, he has never moved far from his singular place, and never in a crowd of people like this. It had to be frightening! We presented him to Yeshua.

"Yeshua. We have brought this blind man to you for healing. His name is Neriah. Will you touch him?"

There was no visage of relief on the man's face standing before The Son of God. He just froze up with his eyes shut so tight it looked as though his eyebrows rested on top of his cheekbones! Yeshua gently took his hand and said…

"Neriah… trust me."

A once ridged and fearful creature softened enough to allow some physical guidance. Yeshua led him through a narrow place between two buildings and set some faithful followers at the opening so no one could pass by. *What was He doing?* A few of us followed Him to a quieter area on the outside of the town. He then turned Neriah around to face Him. Yeshua then put His own spittle on the eyes of the blind man and placed His hands over the eyes and then spoke to Neriah. He took His hands away.

"Neriah… do you see anything?"

Now, as we saw the situation unfold, we were in bewilderment. *Why was Yeshua asking this man if he can see? Normally he would lay His hands on them and they are immediately healed. Does He question His own ability to heal now?* Neriah relaxed and opened his eyes slowly, as if to be afraid of what he might see or not see. Then his face lit up.

"I see men like trees! Walking trees!"

Yeshua put His hands on the man's eyes again and waited for just a moment then pulled them away.

"Now… what do you see?"

"I see! I see again!" Tears spilled down his face as he wept uncontrollably. "Why did you do this for me? I am undeserving of such grace from such a Man of God!"

Yeshua stepped forward and held him until the crying subsided.

"You must understand Neriah, the Fathers love for you is complete and unwavering. You must now put the past behind you and seek The Kingdom of God. In God's Kingdom, we are *ALL* His children. Now go… only to your home. Do not go back into the town and do not tell anyone there what has happened to you."

Neriah thanked Yeshua, then turned to Simon and I and said…

"Thank you for not giving up one me! I was just too afraid of the unknown."

He embraced us then ran for home.

Chapter 32: Temple Tax and a Rich Fish

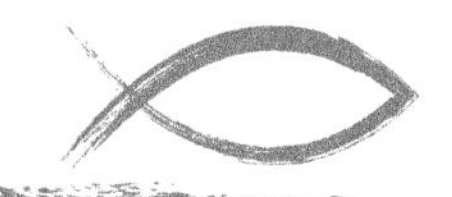

I had reservations about going to Capernaum. I would see Hanna again and I would prefer not to deal with it. The feelings we have for each other is real, but an impossibility. We are from two different times and have two different destinies.

As per usual, word had spread, and we had many spectators to greet us as we entered the small city. Yeshua was ushered into Peter's house to escape the pressing crowd, while Peter stood outside fending off the attack of several children who were excited to see their father again. He fell to the ground under a sea of laughter and abundant kisses. I loved to see the joy on their faces as they tortured him so.

I longed for the feeling of family once more. My own selfish desire wished to stay here and start a family with Hanna. I could easily forget my old life and spend the rest of my life here with her. I felt a gentle touch on my shoulder.

"Benjamin... It's good to see you again so soon."

A soft smile and sorrowful eyes met mine.

"It's good to see you too Hanna."

Our greeting was cut short when Peter nudged us toward the house. His grin was obvious as to what he is thinking. We turned to go in.

"Peter!"

Peter was hailed by two men from the diminishing crowd out front. Peter's contempt for the two men flashed in his eyes when he saw them. Seems as though *a lot* of people in this town irritated Peter.

"Jonathan and Simeon… Why must you ruin my happiness? What do you want of me? I am tired and would like to spend time with my family!"

"Does your teacher not pay the Temple tax?"

"Yes, He does… Why do you ask? We have only just arrived, and you are seeking this?"

"Of course, Peter, this is our duty… Do not find fault in us for doing so."

Peter waved his hand at them, then proceeded to throw both hands in the air in frustration while turning on his heals. Hanna and I stifled a laugh. Peter is always so expressive! We followed him into the house. Without even hearing what went on outside, Yeshua proceeded to question Peter about the exchange he had with the Temple tax collectors.

"What do you think, Simon? From whom do the kings of earth take customs or taxes… from their sons, or from strangers?"

"From strangers, Lord."

"Then the sons are free. Nevertheless, lest we offend them, go to the sea, cast in a hook, and take the fish that comes up first. And when you have opened its mouth, you will find a piece of money; take that and give it to them for Me and you."

Peter hung his head down in a dejected manner. All he wanted to do at this point was see his family, and it kept being delayed. However, he was obedient.

"Yes Lord. I will do as you say."

As the trade ship was sailing away from Capernaum, its bow cut the waves uniformly to either side of the craft. Loaded with merchandise, its center of gravity displaced the ship solidly for a somewhat smooth journey. Some were attending to the riggings, while others focused on more important matters. Gambling. The high stakes game had started before putting out to sea. Five men gathered around two, locked in heated battle. Coins were displayed on the mat as each stake was raised, and cheers from the onlookers incited an adrenaline rush that began to impede fair gambling practices. One of the men exploded in embarrassment for losing and attempted to sweep up the coins in one failed motion.

But one single coin escaped the tightening of his fist and went sailing through the air. Sunlight reflected off the flat sides of the coin as it went spinning into the sea. As the coin broke the surface of the water, it shot down in a swooping angle about ten feet and started spinning once again... shinning like a beacon to all underwater life. Just as a fishing lure is made to attract attention, the bright color and sparkling light was irresistible to the large Tilapia swimming nearby. In a burst of speed, it captured its prize and swam off toward the shore.

Peter stood with his feet in the water; the waves cascading in a sweeping motion over his feet. His hand felt for the line, buried somewhere within his satchel. His fingers felt the familiar, coarse line and a heavy weighted bronze hook. He stopped for a moment to think.

I have no bait... just a line and a hook. He never said to bait it. Just throw in the line. Have faith Peter!

With a measure of faith that Peter was unaccustomed to, he unraveled the line and with the expertise of a seasoned fisherman, cast the line out at its max distance. The dry line floated on the surface, but the weight of the bronze hook began to pull the line under as it descended into the deep. Only a few feet away swam a fish with a miracle in its mouth. From a purse, to a mat, to the sea, to a fish. Dull and lifeless... a bronze hook dropped ever so slowly.

Peter felt a tug on the line.

Chapter 33: Busy Day

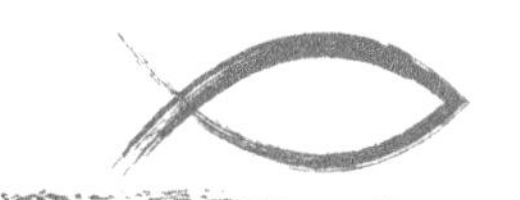

After celebrating the Feast of Tabernacles in Jerusalem. Everyone made their way to Bethany, where Lazarus lived. They were invited to the house of his sister, Martha. The front of the home was rather grand. It had a high wall made of stone with a set of double doors in the center. As they entered the dwelling, Martha made it clear that she was hosting this event.

"Mary! Please see to it that our guest is made comfortable and then come help me prepare some food. I have just the right thing in mind for this special occasion!" Martha bustled off without even greeting her guests. "Mary!"

Mary was so gracious. She greeted each one personally, with a warm smile.

"Come… follow me."

They entered a courtyard with flat stone pavers providing a smooth, transition to all areas of the dwelling. Immediately to the left was a covered stable-like area, housing the common staple of farm animals needed for everyday necessities. Set about the courtyard in strategic places, were cisterns to catch rainwater. Just past the stable, was a kitchen-like area where Martha busied herself. As Mary led them passed the cooking section, Martha kept glancing up. She anxiously searched for a notice of approval. Unfortunately, all eyes were on Mary, for she was leading the group.

At the end of the courtyard was a large opening into the dining room. Inside was a rather large U-shaped, low standing table called a *triclinium*. Yeshua and the disciples were seated, reclining on pillows, while the rest were seated in the courtyard.

Mary was quite captivated by Yeshua. She never took her eyes off Him. As He spoke, she found herself inching ever closer to this Man of God. Without notice, she found herself at His feet, completely engrossed with every word He shared.

Martha was hard at work and wondering where her sister could be. She wanted this dinner to be perfect! *This is a Man of God!* She thought. *Everything must be perfect, and my sister doesn't even have the decency to help me prepare… something must be done about this!* Martha wiped the sweat from her brow, straightened her clothing, then stepped into the dining room. Mary was sitting at the foot of Yeshua. This infuriated her! Trying to stifle her emotion, Mary approached the table. Everyone could see the redness in her face and the expression of disdain she exhibited. She let out an exasperated sigh.

"Lord… do You not care that my sister has left me to serve alone? Tell her to help me!"

There was a momentary hush of conversation as each person recoiled at the tenacity of this woman. Surrounded by deafening silence, she realized the rudeness of her comment. She dropped her chin to her chest in embarrassment. Yeshua smiled.

"Martha, Martha, you are worried and troubled about many things! But one thing is needed… and Mary has chosen that good part, which will not be taken away from her."

Martha, set back by His response, bowed rather awkwardly and withdrew back to the cooking. *How could I have been so foolish!*

Martha placed her face in her hands and wept, too engrossed in self-pity to see Mary approach her.

"Martha." Mary's voice was soft and gentle. "Martha, I'm sorry if I upset you. I only just wanted to hear the words of Yeshua. I've been imagining for so long what He was like, and now He is here to experience for ourselves! His words are so... so life changing! You must come and listen. Do not worry over the food... just come with me." Mary held her hand out to Martha.

"I am too ashamed to go back in there. I acted foolishly! I failed to even *greet* Him when He arrived! I was only concerned with trying to impress Him with my servitude."

"Come Martha."

Mary held out her hand again, then gestured with her fingers for Martha to take hold. Hesitantly, Martha accepted and was led back into the fellowship of Yeshua.

Chapter 34: Our Father...

It was a quiet morning. There was much fellowship deep into the night with Lazarus, Mary, and Martha. Martha was pleased to have finally fed everybody and had learned to be still enough to listen.

Even before sunrise, Yeshua had gone upstairs alone, and was praying. Needing to know what the day would bring, Peter and Andrew sought Him out to plan out the day. Would they be staying here? Would they be moving on? They found their way upstairs and discovered Him praying. Yeshua had spent a lot of time doing this since they had known Him… hours upon hours of it. Peter was curious, waited for Him to finish, then asked

"Lord, You do not pray as the other Rabbis do… and we see the strength that comes from this time spent with the Father. John taught his disciples to pray. Can You teach us to do the same as You?"

"Yes, Peter. I will teach you. You and Andrew wait here while I gather the others."

The rest of the disciples were told to go up to the roof so Yeshua could speak with them privately. I was in the courtyard with Simon enjoying a nice conversation when I noticed Simon's eyes looking behind me. There was someone approaching.

"Ben." I turned and faced Yeshua. "Will you join us on the roof top this morning? There are things I will be teaching that you need to know."

Simon looked at me with an expression of surprise, as if to say *Privileged... aren't we?* I followed the Son of God upstairs. I could feel the warmth of the morning sun on my face now. The sky was blue as can be, with no clouds in sight. This early in the morning, sound carried far. Birds were singing, and the blatting of sheep could be heard in the distance. Sounds of the market were also audible as everyone was setting up for a day of merchandising.

The disciples looked a little surprised at my being present but shrugged it off knowing that Yeshua would have His reasons. I was met with a few smiles. I sat down next to Phillip; he seemed the most accepting of my being there. Yeshua began.

"You must understand something. I am here to restore your relationship with the Father, just as it was meant to be in the beginning. You were meant to have dominion over this earth and to have authority over everything. That is why I say that if you have the faith of a mustard seed, you can move a mountain! When you realize the authority that you have in the Father's Kingdom... *ALL* things are possible! This comes with knowing Him. This comes with *prayer* and *fasting*.

Yeshua began with a prayer known by millions in the world today.

Our Father, who is in Heaven... Holy is Your Name! Your Kingdom come, Your will be done, on earth as it is in Heaven! Give us day by day our daily bread. And forgive us our sin, as we forgive everyone indebted to us. And lead us not into temptation but deliver us from the evil one."

Peter was the first to ask questions.

"Lord, what does this mean?" Yeshua answered

First you must acknowledge the King of the Universe. Worship Him, for He is worthy! His Kingdom is not of this world, but He wishes it to be so. His Kingdom must be established in your hearts and minds. Worship Him...

Pray for His Kingdom to be established here so that *His will* will be done. So that His mind is *your* mind.

Pray for your daily needs to be met. As I have told you before, He feeds the birds of the air... how much more will he do for you? Give, and He will open the floodgates of heaven to you!

Forgive one another and He will forgive you. If you *do* not forgive, He will not forgive you.

Flee temptation and He will provide a way of escape from it. He will give you the power to overcome the evil one. You will have dominion again... you will have power to do even greater things than ME!"

Peter seemed even more confused...

"Yeshua, how can *WE* do greater things than you??"

"When I leave you Peter, a helper will come and give you power to do great things! You must only believe, and the Holy Spirit will give you the power to do many wondrous things! The Father's Kingdom is *not* of this World... therefore, it does not follow what is possible in man's eyes, but of what is possible with God." Yeshua looked straight at me and said "I say again... You are of the Kingdom of God and there is *NOTHING* that you can't do when you have dominion over the things of *this* World!"

One by one, the Disciples fired off more questions. Every voice trailed into obscurity as tunnel vision set in. My thoughts transferred to the future for just a moment. *What power will I have? Can the Holy Spirit do things through me that are greater than Yeshua Himself?*

Religious thinking has taught us that Yeshua is the very Son of God… and WE are not capable of doing such things as He has done! We cannot forgive sins or absolve them… but we can do other things that are greater! We have *neglected* the very words, spoken over us by the Messiah Himself, saying

"You will do greater things…"

As the meeting was breaking up, I walked downstairs and joined Simon. He could not hide his excitement.

"Well? What happened Benjamin?"

"I don't think I can express the depth of what I just learned to you. Just know this, Simon… God has given us great power to do mighty things for the Kingdom. We must only just believe."

Chapter 35: I Was Blind, Now I See

After the Feast of Dedication, we made our way back toward Jerusalem and with each step, my mind was bombarded with questions. You can study The Word for decades and still not begin to understand its mysteries. Thirty minutes with Yeshua, and he practically destroys all the University studies and experience I had achieved in 20 years! When you go to The Source… you can't go wrong! How many studies have been done on The Lord's Prayer over the span of two thousand years? A simple prayer. An *insightful* prayer. If we were to base our prayer life on these simple principles and walk it out in faith… oh what a victorious life we would live!

Though December in Israel averages moderate, cooler temperatures, this morning was unusually cold! I pulled my garments tight around me and tried to shake off the cold. It had rained earlier, and I was wet and shivering. Every breath exhaled were puffs of crystalized moisture from my lungs. Simon appeared miserable as well. Frost had formed around his mouth while stalactites hung off the end of his beard. He shared his frustrations.

"I long for my dry house, with my dry clothes, and my dry bed! Benjamin, I am very pleased to be following Yeshua, but sometimes it can be unbearable! I haven't slept well since we left Lazarus and his family."

"I share your pain Simon."

If he only knew of the comfort I had to leave behind, he would be even more distraught.

We were taking a risk by coming back to Jerusalem. Yeshua's popularity was growing by the day, and it was all we could do to keep from getting trampled to death! As we entered the narrower streets of the city, our party became bottlenecked... and although it was like being in a bumper car, at least there was more body warmth! Finally, the street opened up to a courtyard and we were able to regroup in our perspective companies again. Yeshua and the disciples... us Followers... Truth seekers... Curiosity chasers... Miracle hunters... and the ever-present Naysayers and Backbiters who provided entertainment along the way! Yeshua had stopped up ahead, and a little bit of chatter began to fill the air. Simon and I pushed our way to the front to see what was going on. Sitting up against the wall, next to a thoroughfare into the courtyard, was a blind man calling out for alms. Phillip spoke out first and asked Yeshua,

"Rabbi, who sinned... this man or his parents, that he would be born blind?" Yeshua squatted down in front of the man to his level and answered.

"It was neither this man who sinned, nor his parents; but it was so that the works of God might be displayed in him. We must work the works of Him who sent Me as long as it is day; night is coming when no one can work. While I am in the world, I am the Light of the world."

The blind man sat there with an expression on his face of excitement, fear, hope, and longing... all rolled up into one picture of emotion in his countenance. Yeshua spat in the one patch of dirt in the entire courtyard that seemed to be dry. He worked up a muddy paste in His fingers then gingerly applied moist clay to the eyes of the blind man. If you could look into the eyes of all who beheld this act, you would find inquisitive faces! Why? Why is Yeshua doing this? Why not just proclaim the healing, as He has done consistently up until this moment? The poor man sat there dumbfounded… not really sure what to do.

"Go… and wash your eyes in the pool of Siloam"

As most people had learned by now, Yeshua had always healed instantaneously, other than the blind man in Bethsaida. Why then was this man told to leave the presence of Yeshua and wash in the pool of Siloam? Nevertheless, his friends helped him to his feet and trudged off in the direction of the pool. Yeshua turned and spoke to John. John turned and made his way to me and Simon.

"Go… Follow this man and his friends. Make sure he does as he was told."

Simon and I looked at each other with a little bit of excitement. *Yeshua has asked US to do something for Him!* Simon could not contain himself.

"Benjamin! We are on a mission! Let's not lose the man… come, let us follow him to the pool!"

There was a little difficulty in catching up to the blind man and his friends. I felt like a salmon fighting to get upstream! As we were pushing away from Yeshua, we were caught in a wave after wave of people trying to push their way *toward* Him. Finally, the crowd lessened, and we made our way down a slope that graduated to the steps of the pool. We watched as the men descended the steps of the pool of Siloam and let the man fulfill his destiny. He kneeled, then bent over and splashed water on his face. After a few moments, he sat back against the stone steps. Quiet, unmoving, breathing heavily… he sat there staring straight ahead. His friends could not contain their excitement.

"What do you see?"

"Can you see now? Tell us!"

Tears began to roll down his face and he began to sob uncontrollably. Were they tears of joy… or sadness? His friends pleaded once again.

"Please! Tell us, were you healed? Has nothing changed?"

The sobbing subsided and the evidence of God's healing power was made evident with a loud proclamation.

"I WAS BLIND BUT NOW I SEE!!" He raised up his hands in praise. "Everything is so beautiful! I do not know what I am looking at… but it is BEAUTIFUL! Praise be to HaShem!

I can't imagine being blind from birth and suddenly being able to see! Everything would be so strange looking. Color… shapes… faces. How could you process that? Simon interjected.

"Benjamin, praise be to Hashem! Every time I see this happen; my heart is full!"

"Mine is too…"

As was directed by Yeshua, the *seeing man* and his friends started to make their way back to the courtyard. The man struggled to walk the foreign landscape before him, so his friends guided him arm in arm. Simon and I turned to follow.

"You two!" I felt a strong grip on my arm that turned me around to face a rather large Temple Guard. Another did the same to Simon. "You follow this Yeshua… Yes?" Simon and I looked at each other; anticipating the outcome if we were to say *yes*. I could feel assurance rising up in me.

"Yes… we are with Yeshua!" Simon followed suit.

"Yes… we follow Yeshua, and you have just seen what He can do! Did you see that man healed of his blindness… down there at the edge of the pool?" The guard became angry and tightened his grip on Simons arm and pulled him close to his face.

"I saw only a young fool pretending to be healed and you are a part of this blasphemous display! You are coming with us!"

There has always been a healthy fear of authorities growing up. I've been pulled over a few times for speeding, and just the presence of a uniformed officer instilled a fear in me. They had the power to take away my license… or even my freedom! These Temple Guards however, had the power to do *much* worse! I can't call my lawyer in this situation. I don't get my one free phone call.

As we made our way to the Temple, Simon and I tried to speak but were quickly buffeted upside the head for speaking. I couldn't understand what was happening… all I could do was pray as we made our way up the steps into a side entrance of the Temple. By this time, the sun had been blocked out by an overcast of deep, gloomy clouds. Darkness was barely deterred by the few torches burning just inside the Temple doors. Obviously having just been lit, the creosote smell was overwhelming, and the black suet crystalized in the cool air around us. It collected on the end of my eyelashes and tickled my nose as I breathed in and out. We came to the doorway of a small room where we were forced inside. One guard left us, while the other stayed and kept us waiting for what seemed like hours. Simon and I tried to figure out what was going on but were hushed immediately. After what seemed like an eternity, the lead guard returned, and we were once again on the move. The guards forced us through a maze of corridors that brought us to what seemed, our destination. This wasn't the floor of the Sanhedrin. Yet a trial of sorts was going on. We were stopped just short of entering and forced to kneel by a sharp blow to the back of the knees. The man *on trial* was the young blind man that Yeshua had healed just hours ago. Apparently, he and his friends were intercepted as well.

"How did you receive your site?" A Pharisee said with a snarl.

"He applied clay to my eyes, and I washed, and I see!"

There was an immediate outcry of antipathy by the accompanying Pharisees. One man cried out

"This Yeshua is not from God, because He does not keep the Sabbath!" Still, another shouted,

"How can a man who is a sinner perform such signs?"

The division in the group was obvious, and the elder Pharisee stood up and questioned the man again.

"What do you say about Him, since He opened your eyes?"

The seeing man thought for a moment...

"He is a prophet!"

Again, there was a great tumult amongst the Pharisees. They consulted one another and decided to call for the parents of this young man to come forward. The parents gingerly made their way up to the side of their son and embraced him.

"Is this your son, who you say was born blind? Then how does he now see?" The mother stepped forward and could not contain her delight.

"Yes! We know that this is our son, and that he was born blind; but now he sees, we do not know who opened his eyes!" She turned to face her son as tears streamed down her face. "Ask him; he is of age. He will speak for himself!"

Again... the Pharisees brought the man forward to question him.

"Give glory to God; we know that this man is a sinner!"

The man stepped forward a second time.

"Whether he is a sinner, I do not know, except that I was once blind... now I see!"

"What did He do to you? How did He open your eyes?"

"I told you already and you did not listen; why do you want to hear it again?" Frustration was evident in his voice. "You do not want to become His disciples too, do you?" The elder Pharisee burst out in anger.

"You are His disciple, but we are disciples of Moses! We know that God has spoken to Moses, but as for *this* man, we do not know where he is from!"

"Well... here is an amazing thing, that you do not know where He is from, and yet He opened my eyes! We know that God does not hear sinners; but if anyone is God-fearing and does His will, He hears Him! Since the beginning of time it has never been heard that anyone opened the eyes of a person born blind... If this man were not from God, He could do nothing!"

I was amazed at this young man's ability to school these Pharisees! The elders face shown red.

"You were born entirely in sin, and you are teaching us?" The elder Pharisee scoffed and shouted

"Take this man away from me! Put him outside! Bring the other men in here!"

Immediately, we were jerked up from our kneeling position and forced into the illegal court of the Pharisees. Brought before the make-shift *Judge,* we were again, forced to our knees.

"You are disciples of this... Yeshua? Do you follow Him?"

You could see the anticipation on his face. He was looking for blood, and he was determined to find it. I spoke without hesitation.

"Yes... I am a follower!" Simon blurted out

"Yes... WE are followers!" I continued. "There is nothing unlawful that He has done. Everything has been in accordance with Torah. Why must you persecute Him?"

"Don't you speak to me of Torah! I *KNOW* Torah! You are nothing but a low man following lofty ideas! However, you have stated from your own mouth that you ARE a disciple. You are to be an example to those who wish to follow this false prophet! Guards! Take these men away! Flog them... put them in chains, then we will see if following this Yeshua is worth the cost!"

We were taken away much more forcibly this time. Off to the side of the courtyard, opposite of where we came in, there was a set of narrow stairs winding down to a lower level of the Temple. There was no light but that of the torch carried by the lead guard, casting ominous shadows on the walls. My mind was racing.

Is this really happening... Are we really going to be flogged??

Never in my wildest dreams... or nightmares, have I ever imagined the possibility of being in this position.

As we descended to the depths of the prison, a stench began to fill our nostrils. A putrid, musty odor that seemed to stick to our clothing. It was *awful*! The narrow, stone steps opened up to a small cavernous area with individual cells and small central area. In the center of it was a post with a large metal ring attached to it. My stomach turned. I had never faced such dread. I tried to muster up some faith.

God has me in this... I can get through this. He will give me the strength!

I looked at Simon. He had terror in his eyes... his face was white as a sheet, and he was shaking uncontrollably. I tried to reassure him.

"Simon... be strong! We can get through this! We are not alone"

"Quiet! No talking! Now... which one of you wants to be first?"

"I do!" The guard was shocked at such a quick and outspoken response. "I will go first, but know this; God is my God, and Yeshua is His Son! He speaks of truth and love!"

"Well let's see if He speaks to you while I show you the kind of love that *I* know of!"

I was wrenched from the place I was standing... my garments were ripped off and tossed to the side. A rope was fed through my shackles, then through the metal ring at the top of the post. Two guards then proceeded to pull up the slack and slowly lift me to where my toes just touched the floor. This way, the skin on my back would be taut... and when the whip cuts across the back, the skin will flay open. I prayed as my tormentor, whip in hand, stood silently for a moment; as if cherishing the thought of what he was about to do. His eyes shown wide with eagerness and a crooked, evil smile came across his face.

"Do you still say that this Yeshua is the Son of God?"

The guard stepped closer to me. He tightly worked the leather wrapped around the hard, wooden handle by twisting it firmly in his hand, to where the leather creaked in his grip. Suddenly, there was a crushing blow to the bridge of my nose! The guard had brought down the wooden handle with such force that I thought my head had split open! All I could see was blood filling my eyes. He burst out in laughter.

"Where is your God now, fool?" Simon shouted

"Stop! There is no need for this! We mean no harm, and we have broken no laws... Roman *OR* Hebrew!"

Simon was met with his *own* blow to the head by the other guard. His guard spoke no words and seemed a little less exuberant about excessive beatings. His captain, my tormentor, was just getting started.

"Now, where were we?" I couldn't see anything, but I could hear his footsteps and labored breathing move around behind me. My body tensed as I anticipated the first blow.

After returning to Yeshua, the now seeing man was being accosted by the neighbors that he had grown up around his whole life. Some believed him, yet others even doubted that he was the same man! He was persuaded to go before the Pharisees and show them this miracle. Meanwhile, there were actually some disciples who noticed that Simon and I were missing. Andrew inquired of John.

"John, Benjamin and Simon have not returned... they did not come back with the young man who was healed!"

John thought for a moment and came to the same realization.

"Andrew... Philip, go to the pool and look for them there. Ask anyone if they may have seen them. I feel in my spirit that something is wrong. I will speak with Yeshua. Now go!"

Andrew and Philip took off for the Pool of Siloam while John turned to seek out Yeshua. John grabbed James and told him of the situation, and they approached Yeshua together.

"Lord, Benjamin and Simon have not yet returned from the Pool of Siloam. Yet The young man who was healed did and has already left. I sent Andrew and Philip to fetch them. Yeshua's expression was one of concern and sadness.

"Yes John, they are not here, nor are they at the Pool of Siloam. We must pray for them, for their faith is being tested. Only through prayer will they find their way back."

While anticipating the first strike of the whip, I was overcome with clarity. My mind immediately recalled what my captor had said.

...let's see if He speaks to you while I show you the kind of love that I know of!

The love that came over me for this man was overwhelming! *The kind of love he knows of.* Obviously, this man had never been shown love his whole life. He was full of anger, hate, and emptiness. I said a quick prayer then spoke to the man.

"So... is this the kind of love that your father had shown you growing up? Beatings?"

I couldn't see him behind me, but I noticed the reaction of the Guards standing in front of me. I continued.

"You have never known love, have you? I am saddened that you had to live such a cruel life as a child."

"BE QUIET! You know nothing of my life!"

I could see... like a film playing in my head, his very life. I started to weep.

"Your mother loved you, didn't she?"

Silence.

"But she was beaten to death by your father when you were young, and your life became nothing but a rage filled existence after that."

"How... How do you know this?" He stammered and muttered to himself. "You *cannot* know this... *Nobody* knows about my past! This is impossible! Tell me who told you this or I will cut you open and spill your insides out on the ground!"

He moved around to the front of me and drew out a knife and held it to my belly.

"We will forget about the slow and agonizing beating and move to a quick death if you do not tell me!" The other guards exclaimed,

"This is not what we were ordered to do!"

The guards who were standing behind him stepped forward and attempted to grab hold of him. He easily shook them off and shot them a deadly stare. I felt the knife being pressed more firmly and more deliberately to just below my navel. At the blink of an eye, I could have my entrails spilled out on the floor. I spoke again without any fear.

"Yes, I know what happened, because The Lord has revealed it to me. When you were finally old enough, you took matters into your own hands and murdered your father for what he did to your loving mother. But the pain has never gone away. You still carry it with you now."

Through the blood and sweat in my eyes, I could see the breakdown of his hard exterior. Tears began to well up in his eyes. He said again, but in a much more subtle and quaking voice,

"You cannot know this. I have told *no one*. Did God really show you this... are you a prophet? How..."

"Yes, God has shown me this, but I am no prophet. I think Hashem has placed me here to show you that *love does* exist. I know that you are filled with an emptiness that cannot be filled. You have tried to fill it up with the only thing you ever learned from your father... violence. If you hated your father so much, why have you become like him? Yeshua has taught us that love can overcome all things. You could kill me... in this very moment, but know this... I love you! God loves you! You do not have to live like this anymore!" The knife momentarily broke my skin, then in one sudden motion he swung the knife above my head and cut the rope that was holding me up! I fell to the ground in a shuddering heap. The adrenalin was coursing through my body. The lead guard then proceeded to pull me up to my feet.

"Turn them loose!" The other guards protested.

"What?? We cannot do that!"

"You WILL do that… Now!"

The guards stood there confounded and motionless, so he jerked the keys out of one of the guard's hands and unlocked my shackles. He then proceeded to do the same for Simon. It was as if I were looking at a different man now. A peace had come over him.

"Go now. Go to this Yeshua… Gods favor is upon you and I will not touch God's anointed! Thank you… I… I feel… I feel…" He choked on a sob, cleared his throat and said one more time… "Go!"

Simon and I quickly dressed and passed the guards in the hopes that they would not pursue us… they didn't. Making our way out seemed like a natural progression through the maze of corridors. It was as if we *knew* the way out! Finally, we burst into the cool evening air and started making our way back to the others. I was having trouble seeing so we stopped back at the pool of Siloam and proceeded to clean out my own blinded eyes so I could see.

"There they are!" We heard Andrew shout behind us. "Where have you been? Benjamin, are you injured?"

"Yes, but not as bad as I could have been."

Simon continued the explanation as I finished washing up. Andrew and Phillip were astonished!

"You were in the Temple prison and escaped?" Phillip shook his head in relief. "Benjamin… Can you walk back with us?"

"Yes Phillip, I can walk… I could run and jump and shout just by knowing what God did in that guard's life today! Truly miraculous!" It felt like the right time to proclaim it… so I did. "He will answer…" Simon followed the cue and shouted

"And He will hear!"

Chapter 36: Lazarus

Before we left the city, Yeshua had come close to being stoned. Tensions were rising in Jerusalem and more and more attempts were being made to discredit or destroy Him. It was once more, a welcome change to be outside the chaos of Jerusalem and in the quiet of the countryside. There was still a chill in the air, but not to the extent of being uncomfortable like it was in Jerusalem. Word of our capture by the Temple guards had spread, and Simon and I were made to tell, and retell the tale over and over again!

There were several small fires spread out amongst different clusters of people in our encampment. Some slept… some ate… while still many others shared their own stories and experiences with anyone who would listen. There was a relaxed buzz of excitement in the air. Simon and I were enjoying the warmth of the fire when I noticed two men hastily approaching Yeshua. Simon and Andrew stood up to greet the men. They were servants of Lazarus. Their faces were grimly set with a message of sorrow.

"Lord… Lazarus, whom You love, is sick. We were sent to retrieve You!" Yeshua's response was not expected.

"This sickness will not end in death. It is to be for the glory of God, so that the Son of God may be glorified by it."

Moments later, the servants turned and headed back to the home of Lazarus. Most thought it strange that Yeshua would not go immediately to his friend and heal him. I knew, however, that this would be the last, major miracle He would perform before His crucifixion… the raising of Lazarus from the dead!

Two days passed before Yeshua spoke of the conversation with Lazarus' servants. Yeshua went to the Disciples and finally announced their departure.

"We are going to Judea again."

Peter and the rest, all responded with an air of caution.

"Rabbi, the Jews were just seeking to stone You, and You want to go there again?"

"Are there not twelve hours in the day? If anyone walks in the day, he does not stumble, because he sees the light of this world. But if anyone walks in the night, he stumbles… because the light is not in him. Our friend Lazarus has fallen asleep; but I go, so that I can wake him out of his sleep."

"Lord, if he has only fallen asleep, then he will recover."

"Lazarus is dead, and I am glad for your sakes that I was not there, so that you may believe; but let us go to him."

Not really understanding what Yeshua was talking about, Thomas conferred with the disciples

"Let us go also, so that we may die with Him."

Simon and I walked together per usual.

"It has been more than two days! Is it possible?" Simon thought for a moment. He remembered the raising of the young boy from the coffin. "He has done it before with the boy, but this has been much longer, I'm sure of it!"

I understood what Simon was saying, but I failed to respond because my own mind was wandering… thinking of how amazing it is, that through all the miracles we have witnessed… we still doubt!

"Benjamin!"

"Yes? Forgive me… Yes, it has been longer, but we must realize that there is no time limit on what God can do."

There is really… nothing that He can't do!

Deep inside the confines of my limited faith, there began a spark of understanding. Yeshua said

Greater things will YOU do than me!

We, as human beings, cannot seem to grasp the infinite possibilities available to us through true, and honest faith. *Greater things…* than raising people from the dead? Greater than walking on the water, or feeding five thousand plus people??? Why is it, that after two thousand years, there has not been but a small handful of people who have experienced such miraculous things? I am beginning to realize that Satan has succeeded very well in distracting believers with a lot of useless pastimes. How much time each day is spent on our knees? Not enough.

Bethany was only about a two-mile walk, so we arrived within an hour or so. Not far from the house, word came to us that Lazarus had been in the tomb four days already. Many of the Disciples were beginning to cry. Overwhelming grief in the community was apparent. Lazarus was well loved! Martha approached us.

"Lord, if You had been here, my brother would not have died! But even now, I know that whatever You ask of God, He will do for You!" Yeshua embraced Martha to comfort her.

"Your brother will rise again."

"Yes, Lord... I know that he will rise again in the resurrection on the last day."

"I... am the resurrection and the life; he who believes in Me will live even if he dies, and everyone who lives in Me will never die! Do you believe this?"

"Yes Lord... I have believed that You are the Messiah, the Son of God, even He who comes into the world."

"Martha. Where is your sister?"

"I will get her."

Martha turned and ran into the village, pushing her way through the crowd of mourners that had accumulated outside and inside the house.

"Mary! Mary! Come quickly!"

Mary was startled at Martha's shout, but was soon relieved when she came to the realization as to why Martha was so excited... and *smiling*! She respectfully shook off those who were consoling her and embraced her sister.

"Is He really here Martha? Has He finally come?"

"He waits for you... go!"

Mary quickly exited the house, with the *mourning* entourage on her heels. She has been so overwhelmed with everything that has happened, and the delay in Yeshua's arrival had intensified her feelings of loss. She just *knew* that He would make everything all right again!

Mary found Yeshua and fell at His feet, crying.

"Lord, if only You had been here, my brother would not have died!"

Yeshua was moved with such compassion. There were so many people gathered who love Lazarus and were *truly* grief stricken! He knelt down and laid a gentle hand on Mary's shoulder.

"Where have you laid him?"

Mary looked up into the crying eyes of Yeshua. She paused for a split second and just stared into the ocean of love that exuded from His eyes. *Everything will be all right.*

"Come and see."

Mary and Martha led the way.

As most people do, some individuals followed along and began to criticize Him for not being around when He was needed, while still some exalted Him for how much He loved Lazarus.

Inside the tomb of Lazarus, it was pitch black, quiet... Nothing moved but a few beetles exploring the cracks and crevasses of the tomb. They scurried precipitously on the walls and floors of the cave... antennae flitting about, sensing the decaying flesh within the cool confines. They are carrion beetles of the Silphidae family; mostly responsible for the consumption of many loved ones throughout the centuries. The careful mix of myrrh and aloes were warding off the insects for now, but as the odor of the spices dissipated... they would soon feast.

The beloved brother of Mary and Martha lay motionless on a slab of stone. He had been carefully washed and then wrapped in strips of spice-laden linen. Within the tightly wrapped linen, lay a lifeless body. Cold to the touch... and by this time, rigor mortis had set in the joints. Also, blood had drained to the bottom half of the body because of gravity. Flesh had begun to break down and liquify. Lazarus was surely dead, there was no doubt.

There was a cracking noise... Startled, the family of beetles scurried about trying to find the nearest hiding place available, running over, under, and around each other in a panic. There was a crack in the darkness as well. Sunlight shot through the tomb like a focused laser. The thin ray of sunshine slowly widened as the stone was rolled to the side of the opening. Dust particles refracted light throughout the cave, looking like gold dust floating down from the ceiling. Still no movement.

"Lazarus!"

Microscopic, electrical impulses shot through every cell of the body, solidifying tissue and restoring life to the muscle and joints. The room began to echo with an ever so slow, and faint heartbeat…

"Lazarus!"

The heartbeat accelerated to a regular sinus rhythm and a gasp of air was pulled through the wrappings around the mouth of Yeshua's friend.

"Lazarus! Come out!"

Lazarus woke in a panic! *Had he fallen asleep?? Why couldn't he breath very well? Why couldn't he see?* All of these thoughts materialized in a split second until he realized that he was wrapped in linen and was overwhelmed with the pungent smell of Myrrh. He remembered now… he was deathly ill. Could it be? Could he really *have died and was buried??*

Lazarus pulled at the linen wrapped around his face as best he could with his constricted, linen bound hands. He managed to free up a space over one eye so he could see; and proceeded to shuffle his way toward the opening of the tomb. He could have sworn he heard his friend Yeshua's voice calling to him. As he neared the entrance, the light was blinding! He held up one hand to shield the sun from his exposed eye... and continued to lumber right out of his sepulcher.

The small multitude gathered around the tomb gasped! Yeshua really did it! He raised Lazarus from the dead! Yeshua smiled.

"Unbind him and let him go!"

Mary and Martha ran up to Lazarus and about knocked him over with their embrace! They proceeded to remove the shroud of death he was wrapped in. As they unwound the linen… a healthy Lazarus was exposed. Someone handed them a garment to cover him. Many, many people came to believe in the Messiah that day and there was much celebration well into the evening!

Chapter 37: A Conversation with Yeshua

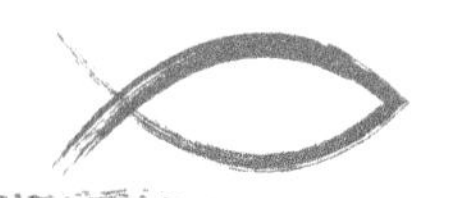

Having experienced much, these past years traveling with Yeshua... there was no way I'd ever be the same again! How could I be? To see, firsthand, the miracles... to hear the teachings of Yeshua without the filter of translation... or to experience personally, *His* great love... priceless! He captivates people like I have seen no other do, and the written Word of God comes nowhere close to expressing His attributes!

Deep in thought, my eyes were locked on the horizon without even seeing it. A shadow moved in front of me, breaking my introspection. Yeshua smiled and sat down beside me. I didn't want this conversation. I knew in my spirit what it would be about.

"Benjamin... I will ask you the same question I asked you when we first met. Why do you think you are here?"

My opinions were many, yet a solid answer could not be found, but I tried to reason it out.

"Lord, I thought in the beginning, that it was to heal me from the brokenness I had concerning my family. Then, I thought it was to re-establish my heritage and become a Rabbi... or something to that effect. But now, I only know that my heart is broken because I don't want to leave. I have a true understanding of who *You* are... and who the *Father* is, and there is nothing I want more than to serve Him as You have. I want to see *His Kingdom* established on this earth in the way that You have shown us. I truly do not know why I am here, only that I do not want to leave."

My heart was in my throat, and the backdrop in front of me began to liquify as the tears formed up in my eyes. I have never known such loss as I was feeling in this moment.

"Ben, I will be with you always. This is not the end, but only the beginning." His eyes consoled me. "You know what is coming for Me… just as the Father has deemed it so, but this world will not truly take hold of the *Kingdom* message for many years. Just as the birds come and steal the grain sown by the wayside, so will the enemy come to take this message from those that do not understand it and misinterpret it to lead them from its true meaning. Remember what I said before;

I speak to them in parables, because seeing they do not see, and hearing they do not hear, nor do they understand."

"But Yeshua, what am *I* to do? For what purpose does the Father have me here… and what am I to do when I return? I am nobody special. I am no disciple, or apostle. I am just a professor from Pennsylvania!"

"There will always be remnants of the Kingdom, and there will always be those who love and serve the Father. In *your* time, many have remained faithful, but are still deceived. They are not living to the full purpose of what God intended for their lives. They live in defeat and poverty of life. They lack self-discipline and passion. This should not be so! They need to be reminded of who they are in *The Kingdom of God*! They will be a mighty force against the enemy when they finally realize what power they hold! The Harvest will be ripe once again to hear and receive the message of the *Kingdom*. My Father has seen a gift in you that will enable you to teach and disciple people into the Kingdom along with many others that will come along side of you. My message has been to restore what has been taken away. Relationship with the Father, and dominion on this earth. The Harvest will be plentiful, but many tares are found among the wheat. The Holy Spirit will guide you, and others, and will give you power to *do greater things than I have done*! I would not say this, if it were not from the Father. Don't be deceived! Listen to the Holy Spirit... *always*! Follow my example and you will do well... I have faith in you Ben!"

This was too much! My head was swimming.

"Lord, I will do as you say... but I am so unworthy!"

"That is why you have been chosen. A true leader is one who teaches others to replace him in the work that he does. As I have shown you... so do."

"How do I go back? *When* do I go back?"

"Tomorrow, you will journey to the place where you arrived. Find rest there, and you will be returned."

"I don't want to leave you!"

Yeshua embraced me as I wept.

I said goodbye to a few of the Disciples, such as Andrew and Phillip and looked over the rest of this traveling group of visionaries. I will miss all of them. Peter, and his rough exterior but heart of mush... Matthew, with his calculated expressions but willingness to follow anyway... James and John, who strived for power and position but loved, nonetheless. Without sharing the details, I asked Simon to accompany me to Capernaum. Then I would go on to the Golan Heights alone. As expected, Simon had many questions.

"Why must you leave now? I do not wish you to go my friend! Where are you going?"

"I am returning home... Yeshua has said it is time, so I must leave. Simon, you will be remembered as one of my dearest friends! You have been so patient with me and have helped guide me to a place of peace and a meeting with Yeshua. I do not wish to leave... I have grown to love you as my own brother."

"As have I, Benjamin! I do not wish you to leave! I must say, you have been the most curious and wonderful friend I have ever known!" Simon stifled a nervous laugh. "However, you must do as Yeshua bids you to do. You, as well, are like a brother to me and I will never forget you!"

Simon quickly grabbed ahold of my garment and pulled me to him in a strong embrace and kissed me on both cheeks. Stepping back, he brushed aside his tears and grinned that silly grin that I had grown to love.

"Well Benjamin... let us travel together as we once did in the beginning. What a time we have had! What a life we have been able to witness!"

Chapter 38: The Journey Home

Stocking up with some food and trying to keep a low profile was difficult, but Simon and I managed to slip away without much notice from those who were not informed. The first few miles were trod in silence. Escaping this sorrow would be difficult. Aside from Yeshua, Simon has been the closest friend to me that I have ever known. We have lived literally, side by side now, for almost three years.

"Ben... Where is it that you live? You have never *really* explained it to me. I have not travelled to many countries, but I *do* know of them through study and people I have met. Why do you never speak of it?"

I was really quite surprised that Simon had managed to keep a lid on his curiosity concerning my place of origin these past years. Not once, has he brought it up... until now. He deserved at least a *partial* explanation.

"Remember how I said my family was originally from Israel?"

"Yes."

"Before I was born, they moved far away to a country that can only be reached by ship. It is a three-month journey across the sea."

"That is not possible! No one has travelled that far!"

Simon was a little indignant. He considered himself to be a learned man and found this idea to be extremely farfetched!

However, he still showed a little restraint with his emotions on this. Everything he has ever known to be *normal* has been put into question since meeting Yeshua. We stopped walking and faced one another.

"Yes… it seems impossible, but Simon, God brought me here! I didn't come on a ship; I just woke up here the day before I met you. I can't explain it. It just happened."

"You just woke up here?" Simon chewed on that statement for a moment. "Nothing *is* impossible with God! Truly… Nothing!"

That silly grin, once again, took hold of his countenance and he let out a nervous laugh while shaking his head.

"You are an *ODD* man Benjamin Messler!"

Four days later, we arrived at Simons home. Once again, I found myself on a balcony overlooking an olive orchard. This time the sunset was stark and grey… and there was no sweet fragrance lingering in the air. The trees did not shiver with delight. They now lay dormant without color... without life. Such a fitting end to an epic journey. As with seasons of change, God allows times of growth, and times when we must be still and listen.

I'm listening Father… and I will obey.

There was a knock at the door.

"Come in!"

Simon stepped through the doorway… hands folded behind his back. Each step purposed and careful.

"Will you return the same way you came here? Will you wake up and find yourself back home?" There was such a sadness in his voice. "Will you forget me?"

His voice trailed off with a faint sob while tears welled up in his eyes. I was about to lose it myself!

"Simon… of course not! I could never forget you! You *are*, and *always* will be my closest friend! You are my brother!"

We embraced. We cried. We said our goodbyes.

Chapter 39: Home Again

I woke up. I didn't open my eyes though… I was afraid to. I could feel the difference in the atmosphere around me and I could *smell* the difference too. I braced myself for the reality I now found myself in. I opened my eyes. The room was dimly lit because of the drawn curtains, but I could see that I was back home. A flood of emotions burst out of me as I leaned over and put my head in my hands. I wept uncontrollably for least a good ten minutes!

Why must I be here Lord?

I prayed for strength.

If it could be called a dream, I would call it that. If it could be called an episode of Psychotic Dementia… I'd call it *that*! But it wasn't. Questions began to race in my mind.

Was what happened real? What proof do I have… other than what I felt in my spirit? Then I remembered.

I looked down and beheld my ancient clothing. My outer garment, tunic and belt… No flannel or blue jeans. I pulled my garment away from my chest and looked for the scars; the five puncture wounds on each side of my chest. *They were there!* It wasn't a dream! It *was* real!

Now what? Yeshua said that I had a calling on my life for *this* time and that I would know what it is. I had been cooped up in this apartment for months *BEFORE* my journey to the past had even begun. Even then... I had had *NO* outside information. I had no idea where to begin . . . I just wanted to go back. This present world seems so foreign to me now. As I look around at the room, I am surprised at the amount of excess I had accumulated over the years; things of no heavenly value whatsoever. Just empty gratification, that's for sure.

I took a better look at my surroundings. *Wow! What a mess!* There was trash everywhere! How could I live with this? I stood to my feet and got busy cleaning up. As I worked my way around the room filling up trash bags, I found the empty bottle of Scotch and pills. *I should be dead.* With every fiber of my being, I *knew* that I should be dead... yet here I am. I am alive! As I closed my eyes, I could see His face . . . I could *still* feel His presence. He said that He would be with me and I knew it to be true.

"I love you Yeshua!" I whispered. "I am Yours... Please let Your Holy Spirit guide me!"

As I bent down to pick up the empty bottle of Scotch, my arm knocked the TV remote off the end table and onto the floor. I stared at it for a moment then picked it up. Searching its strange functions, I found what I once knew to be the power button and turned it on. I have always had my bills and utilities paid by draft from my banking account, so all of my necessities were still in operation even after all this time.

The Television blared loudly in my ears and the language was almost foreign to me. I had been speaking and hearing the Aramaic language for almost three years in Israel's past. English was hard to process at first, but it didn't take long to comprehend it again. Of course, I had left it on a news channel, and by the looks of things... the state of the country was not good. By the date on the screen, I deducted that I had been away only for about three months in the present time.

Things had heated up in the Middle East. Russia was making moves in the area by allying with Syria and Iran, while America was experiencing civil unrest.

". . . Now we will here from our WGN News correspondent Dan Wimberly – Dan?"

"Thanks Geoff, tensions are high here at the White House. As you can see behind me, people are holding up signs and demanding to know what the state of our country is in and how long President Cowen and the United Alliance Party will be enacting Marshal Law! I have with me a Mr. Richard Cooper of New York. Mr. Cooper, what is it you are trying to accomplish here?"

"We are here asking for answers! We find it hard to believe that the President and this new ***United Alliance Party*** *can just get away with taking over our country without full Congressional approval! It's a Dictatorship! We want answers! They have done away with our Constitution and we want answers!"*

"Thank you, Mr. Cooper . . . Geoff, as we you can see.... tensions are running VERY high right now! Blackwater and U.N. Security Forces have been out in large numbers trying to squelch the outrage that is rising up in most American citizens."

"Dan, can you tell us if the White House has made any statements yet? We are in the dark on this end."

"Yes Geoff, they let us know this morning that President Cowen is meeting with UN officials to solidify the transformation of the United States into the American Nation States. The U.S., Canada, Mexico and South America will become one very large Nation! The Whitehouse Press Secretary has stated that in light of recent events,

this induction will be fast-tracked, and we should hope to be under NWO authority by the first of the month."

"Thank you, Dan . . . Now, experts say that the recovery of the Stock Market is expected to be a slow process, if any gain at all, due to the recent economic collapse we've just experienced . . ."

I clicked off the TV and stood there staring at the blank screen. I never realized how close we were to the end. I remember Yeshua speaking about this, and I have read about this very thing in Matthew, chapter 24. Now that it's happening, a kind of sorrow fills my heart because of the turmoil and tribulation that is being released on an unsuspecting people.

Most Christians have always believed that the rapture would take them out of all this. When it comes to tribulation... I have always thought that American Christians have lived in a protective bubble. People in other countries, even today, have been tortured and beheaded for their beliefs! Most of the *disciples* were tortured and killed for their beliefs! Why should the U.S. be any different? *Here*... If someone so much as gives you a dirty look or a hard time at work because of your belief in God, that *that* is tribulation! How many will be ready to handle this now? Still, I know that God has purposed it that way. *How do I begin? Where do I start?* I started within the walls of my home first.

I stacked the last of the trash bags in the kitchen, then decided to get *myself* cleaned up. There was a rank smell following me around the apartment. Upon further investigation, I realized it was me!

I headed for the bathroom and stopped in the doorway. Straight ahead of me was the toilet... the commode... the porcelain throne! After spending all those times behind trees and bushes, using fig leaves instead of toilet paper, I treasured the thought of modern necessities!

I looked to the left and beheld a stranger in the mirror. I hadn't paid that much attention to my reflection in a long while… and of course my clothing was not the typical daily wear either. My hair and beard had grown out a lot and was unkempt and greasy. *How could I have let myself go this far?* I striped off my garments and beheld a much thinner, fit man! Next, I opened the drawer and pulled out my beard trimmer and razor. *Would I recognize the face behind all of this mess?*

I went to work cutting away my *Grizzly Adams* look and finally began to recognize a familiar face. Then, I pressed the button on my shaving cream and a pungent smell escaped the nozzle. The odor was almost overpowering! I smoothed the foam over my face and went to work with the razor. I felt each whisker catch as I pulled the blade down the side of my face and heard the familiar scrapping sound of the razor against the overgrowth. I could feel the cool air hit my pores as my skin was laid bare. Soon, Ben Messler was standing before me… a younger looking version that was in *great* need of a haircut! I felt strange without the beard though… perhaps I will grow it back.

It was then that I noticed my eyes. They were no longer dark, sad or empty. There was now, evidence of life… peace… and contentment. My eyes started to fill up with tears. God has done such a work in me! I was so thankful to be alive and serving Him. *Thank you, Father!*

I turned the shower on and felt for the right temperature; stepped in and felt the hard spray on my skin. I had to say it again

"Thank you, Father!"

The warm water hitting my skin was like a little piece of heaven. I never thought I could miss such a common, everyday routine. *Man! This feels sooo good!* I grabbed my shampoo and expected a wonderful, smooth lather to attack my hair. Instead, it barely sudsed up! This was going to need a few go-rounds of the wash-rinse-repeat cycle. It took three tries before the lather even showed up! I left the last one on for a few minutes... savoring the tingling sensation.

I turned the hot water all the way up and let it blast my body. The heat was so therapeutic and cleansing. I breathed the steam deep into my lungs and just stood there like that until the water started to turn cold. I quickly rinsed off and dried myself. Next, clean underwear, not an *undergarment*, underwear! Who thought I could be so giddy about underwear? Then... the fresh, clean, now looser fitting clothing. It was actually nice to feel normal again!

I walked through my dimly lit home to the front door. I found my keys and wallet sitting in a basket on the entryway table... just where I left them, many, many months ago.

I stood before a door to a new life... a new adventure, to be sure. Walking through that doorway will be a symbol of my obedience to Yeshua and to the Father. An appointed Covenant between us. Once over that threshold, there will be no turning back! No matter what trial I face... no matter what horrors I see,

I will not back down Lord! You have called me to disciple those who are searching for the Truth! You have called me to proclaim and teach The Kingdom of God. Let Your Holy Spirit guide and protect me and give me the power to do greater things!

I carefully opened the door and stepped into my *True Calling*.

Breath Ben... just breathe.

... to be continued

About the Author

Michael Kohler became a believer at the age of 16... It was then that the creative gifts that God had given him were brought to life. He has spent most of his life centered around the area of music, where singing and song writing were his main focus throughout the years. He majored in Music while attending a Bible School in the Northwest. He has always had a passion for leading Worship; however, creative writing has always been its equal! Life circumstances prevented this book from coming to fruition, but now it's a reality! Michael now resides in North Carolina with his two teenage boys.

The Follower is now available online in most fine bookstores in the U.S.

More information is available by visiting:
www.thefollowerseries.com
or by emailing us at:
thefollowerseries@gmail.com
Also follow us on Instagram @authormichaelkohler

CPSIA information can be obtained
at www.ICGtesting.com
Printed in the USA
BVHW071947151221
624018BV00004B/419

9 781631 290251